TARGET TWO

(THE SPY GAME—BOOK 2)

JACK MARS

Jack Mars

Jack Mars is the USA Today bestselling author of the LUKE STONE thriller series, which includes seven books. He is also the author of the new FORGING OF LUKE STONE prequel series, comprising six books; of the AGENT ZERO spy thriller series, comprising twelve books; of the TROY STARK thriller series, comprising five books; and of the SPY GAME thriller series, comprising six books.

Jack loves to hear from you, so please feel free to visit www.Jackmarsauthor.com to join the email list, receive a free book, receive free giveaways, connect on Facebook and Twitter, and stay in touch!

ISBN: 978-1-0943-8059-9

BOOKS BY JACK MARS

THE SPY GAME
TARGET ONE (Book #1)
TARGET TWO (Book #2)
TARGET THREE (Book #3)
TARGET FOUR (Book #4)
TARGET FIVE (Book #5)
TARGET SIX (Book #6)

TROY STARK THRILLER SERIES
ROGUE FORCE (Book #1)
ROGUE COMMAND (Book #2)
ROGUE TARGET (Book #3)
ROGUE MISSION (Book #4)
ROGUE SHOT (Book #5)

LUKE STONE THRILLER SERIES
ANY MEANS NECESSARY (Book #1)
OATH OF OFFICE (Book #2)
SITUATION ROOM (Book #3)
OPPOSE ANY FOE (Book #4)
PRESIDENT ELECT (Book #5)
OUR SACRED HONOR (Book #6)
HOUSE DIVIDED (Book #7)

FORGING OF LUKE STONE PREQUEL SERIES
PRIMARY TARGET (Book #1)
PRIMARY COMMAND (Book #2)
PRIMARY THREAT (Book #3)
PRIMARY GLORY (Book #4)
PRIMARY VALOR (Book #5)
PRIMARY DUTY (Book #6)

AN AGENT ZERO SPY THRILLER SERIES
AGENT ZERO (Book #1)
TARGET ZERO (Book #2)
HUNTING ZERO (Book #3)
TRAPPING ZERO (Book #4)

FILE ZERO (Book #5)
RECALL ZERO (Book #6)
ASSASSIN ZERO (Book #7)
DECOY ZERO (Book #8)
CHASING ZERO (Book #9)
VENGEANCE ZERO (Book #10)
ZERO ZERO (Book #11)
ABSOLUTE ZERO (Book #12)

PROLOGUE

An isolated farmhouse somewhere near Durham, northern England
2 a.m.

Nothing in Professor Arnold Woburn's long years of study had prepared him for this.

For forty years, he had meticulously learned Ancient Hebrew and Ancient Greek, studied the Old and New Testaments, and worked at his skills as a translator, historian, and Bible commentator. He could speak five modern languages in addition to the two dead ones, scan an archaeological site to find the most likely spots to excavate, and hold a roomful of scholars in the palm of his hand as he enumerated his latest discoveries.

But he had never, ever had to deal with a roomful of thugs intent on beating the crap out of him.

And they still hadn't told him why they would even want to.

They had abducted him as he drove back from a late-night lecture at the University of Durham where he was a Visiting Professor of Theology, on a six-month sabbatical from the University of North Carolina-Chapel Hill. He'd been driving along a rural lane outside of town, not two miles from his house, thinking through the lecture he needed to give the next day when a van a hundred yards ahead of him slammed on the brakes and turned to block the street. A car driving behind him did the same, hemming him in.

As he sat there, dumbly trying to figure out what was going on, several men rushed from both vehicles, hauled him out of his car, and hustled him into the back of the van. Before he was fully aware of what was happening, he'd been blindfolded, handcuffed, and thrown on the floor of the van.

As the van pulled away, he'd cried out, "I'll give you whatever you want. Take me to an ATM and I'll withdraw—"

A punch to the stomach was the only instruction he needed to keep quiet.

The rest of the long ride was made in utter silence.

When the van finally opened and the blindfold was taken off, he found himself inside a large garage. The other car was parked in the second bay. The men who had abducted him wore no masks, which frightened him more than anything they could have said or done.

They didn't care if he saw their faces because he'd never get to tell anyone.

Why? Why? He kept going over the question in his mind as they hustled him into the house, through a spacious and well-appointed living room, and down into a cellar. Why would these men abduct him? He wasn't rich. He wasn't famous beyond a small circle of academics. He didn't have access to state secrets. Neither did his wife. What could this all be about?

He was too afraid to ask, too afraid to open his mouth.

They stood him in the middle of the concrete cellar, a single bare bulb dangling just above his head. He counted eight of them, all young or early middle age. All with hard features and pitiless eyes.

They took the cuffs off. He stood there, looking nervously about him, rubbing his chafed wrists.

Someone behind him cleared his throat.

Professor Woburn turned, thinking one of these thugs was finally going to talk to him.

Instead, he received a slap on the face.

The professor staggered back, more surprised than hurt. The slap hadn't been all that hard, just so unexpected.

"What do you—"

Another man slapped him, harder this time. Woburn staggered again, then got slapped by a third man.

The circle closed on him.

He covered his head, and the slaps turned to punches against his stomach, back, and ribs.

All of those punches were pulled. He could tell that any of his eight abductors could have floored him with a single blow. At sixty-eight, it had been a long time since he had done any real exercise, and all of these men were in good shape.

"Why are you doing this to me?" he wailed as the blows increased in tempo but not in strength.

Even so, the pain began to overwhelm him. His knees buckled, and he ended up crouched on the floor, shoulders hunched, with his arms over his head for protection.

A sharp whistle. The blows stopped.

For a moment, Woburn didn't move, thinking it was some sort of trick.

Then he dared to peek through his fingers.

An older man in a business suit, features sharp under a shaved head, walked across the cellar and stopped in front of him, studying him with icy blue eyes.

He gave a nod, and Woburn's abductors began to hit him again.

Woburn cried out in pain and confusion.

After a few more seconds of abuse, the newcomer whistled again. The blows stopped.

Woburn looked up at the man in command.

"Hello professor. I will ask you questions, and you will answer them, fully and without hesitation. Do you understand?"

The accent had a Midwestern twang. Indiana, maybe further west. But refined. This was no farmer, but an educated man who hadn't given up his roots.

Professor Woburn nodded.

"Very well. You were on the Tel Shimon excavation in 2015, weren't you?"

"Y . . . yes," he replied, confused. Why would a group of thugs want to know about that?

"And the excavators found a sealed clay jar containing papyri, didn't they?"

"Yes, but why—"

Blows rained down on him. Woburn curled up again. The man whistled, and the blows stopped.

"I ask the questions, Professor Woburn, not you. You were the epigrapher for the excavation, and you made the initial translation of the papyri, which were written in Ancient Hebrew."

Realization began to dawn.

"That's correct," Woburn said reluctantly.

"What did they say?"

Woburn almost asked why in the world someone would kidnap and beat him in order to discover what he had read on ancient papyri almost ten years ago.

But the question caught in his throat as fear clenched down around it.

Not fear of getting another beating for speaking out of turn, but because he realized what these people were after.

The man in charge slapped him again. "What did they say?"

"Y . . . you want to know about the Ark."

"Obviously. Answer."

"But these are legends. You have to understand that in the time of King Solomon—"

Another slap. "I'm not interested in your interpretation. Tell me what they said."

"The papyri said the Ark of the Covenant was buried under the Temple of Solomon."

This would have been laughable if these people weren't so in earnest. Two-thousand-year-old bits of Israelite political propaganda and they thought they were real?

This is what Colonel Haddad had been talking about when he confiscated the papyri and forbade him from publishing.

"I'm sorry your work will come to nothing, professor, but if this gets out, every eccentric and treasure hunter in the world will try to dig under the Temple Mount. It's an explosive enough site as it is. We can't have that."

Woburn had understood. The mound in the center of Old Jerusalem was the site of King Solomon's temple, which was destroyed by the Babylonians in 587 BC. It was rebuilt a few decades later as the Second Temple, and it stood until it was destroyed again by the Roman general, and future emperor, Titus in 70 AD. Only the Western Wall of the Second Temple remained visible. Often called the Wailing Wall, it was the most sacred spot for Jews, who came from all over the world to pray there.

Right on top of the hill above the Western Wall stood the Dome of the Rock, one of the holiest sites in Islam, where Mohammed took a winged steed up to Heaven. The only holier pilgrimage centers were Medina and Mecca. The Jews and Muslims had been fighting over the Temple Mount for centuries, and with the establishment of Israel, that fight had only gotten worse. Barely a year went by without some serious bloodshed on the site.

To have treasure hunters digging there would be like throwing a flare into an oil well.

"Did they specify where?" the man in the business suit asked.

Professor Woburn could never forget when he first translated that revelatory line. It was burned in his memory forever.

"They were vague. The exact line was, 'The Pharisees went beneath the Temple of Solomon, into the Tunnels of the Holy, and secreted the sacred Ark there to keep it safe from the enemies of the Lord.'"

"Did they mention anything else about the tunnels?"

"No. The papyri were written during the Bar Kokhba rebellion in the 130s AD. The style of writing and language, and the pot they were found in, point to that same century. Mostly the writing was about the rebellion itself, as well as some day-to-day affairs of worship. It was all published."

"I know, professor. I read your publication. But the key text, the one you just quoted, was never published. Why not?"

Woburn wanted to ask how this man even knew about it. So few did. But it wasn't his place to ask questions. He had learned that now.

"The Israeli government confiscated it and said that if I published, people would try to dig into the Temple Mount. Even if we point out that it's just propaganda from a later century, people will still think it's real and hunt for it. And you can't even try!" he blurted, forgetting his place. "Think of the political chaos that would cause. And the security there is ironclad. There are soldiers and cameras everywhere. If you try, you'll get arrested or, worse, shot. You might even get lynched!"

Woburn stopped himself, realizing he had spoken out of turn. And yet, he hadn't been struck. The businessman smiled at him.

"Arrested? Lynched? I don't think so, professor. Oh, the Temple Mount is well guarded, yes, but we've been planning this for a long time. We thought this might be the place, and we only needed you to confirm it."

But how did they even know about it? He was the only one who had even read the thing, except for Moshe, the graduate student at Hebrew University who was his assistant on the dig, and he had died in a car wreck last year.

Oh, wait. He hadn't died in a crash at all, had he?

Woburn's throat constricted. He tried to speak, but his words only came out as a croak. He cleared his throat and tried again.

"Wait. Please, I—"

There was a flash of movement coming down in front of his face. Something constricted around his throat. He scratched at it and felt a thin metal wire. His eyes bugged as the wire cut through flesh. A knee in the small of his back made him arch his spine. He pulled on the wire, cutting his own fingers in a desperate attempt to push it away and get another lungful of precious air.

The businessman still stood in front of him, showing no reaction at all.

“Thank you for your assistance, Professor Woburn. We’ve given you a great honor. Instead of merely studying history, you will now be a part of making history.”

A minute later, Professor Arnold Woburn was dead.

CHAPTER ONE

Marrakech, Morocco
Noon
That same day

Jacob Snow bided his time, waiting for the target to make the first move. He'd been sitting at a food stall in the vast plaza of Jemaa al-Fna in Marrakesh for half an hour now, watching Karim ibn Mohammed eating a steaming bowl of *harira*, a Moroccan soup made with tomato and chickpeas. They guy was eating slowly, savoring it as much as he savored torturing captives on the Dark Web.

Dubbed the "Master of Pain" in various online forums, Karim ibn Mohammed was a Dark Web celebrity. He'd killed numerous so-called "enemies of Islam," including a cop in some hick Moroccan town down south who had the audacity to arrest one of Karim's operatives.

That video had lasted fifteen minutes. The Moroccan cop, an old guy who looked like he had spent most of his career issuing parking tickets, lived until the very last second.

Jacob had forced himself to watch. Unlike what a lot of people thought, CIA operatives don't get desensitized to sights like that. Well, Jacob had to admit that they do get desensitized a little. It was the only way for the mind to survive the onslaught, but the spirit didn't get desensitized. Every time he saw one of Karim's videos, his faith in humanity died a little more.

And after watching all those videos, he was now watching the star of the show, eating his soup without a care in the world.

Jacob would make him care soon enough. By the end of the afternoon, the Master of Pain would be in a very dank, dark jail cell. Or he'd be dead.

Jacob knew which fate he'd prefer for the barbarian.

The Jemaa al-Fna was the perfect place to hide in plain sight, and the perfect place to stalk a terrorist. The huge square, bounded by old buildings and the city's main mosque, throbbed with activity.

The center was taken up by dozens of food stalls serving everything imaginable. Grills sent up waves of heat into the air already seared by the African sun and gave off rich smells of lamb, chicken, and goat. Vast, steaming pots full of soup added to the smells and heat. Blenders whirred to pulp fruit for juice, and knives *rat-tat-tatted* against cutting boards, sounding like machine guns as chefs hurriedly diced vegetables for the next hundred *tajines*.

Surrounding this food market were open, but not empty, areas. Here traditional storytellers stood on chairs, recounting ancient tales to captivated audiences of robed and hooded Moroccans. A puppet show nearby entertained a gaggle of open-mouthed children, and beyond that, a gaggle of tourists, equally openmouthed, watched a grizzled old snake charmer do tricks with an Indian rat snake, a perfectly harmless species whose main defense mechanism is to look like a cobra.

Jacob got bitten by a real cobra once when on assignment in Pakistan. He didn't blame the old coot for playing with a fake one. Jacob still had the scar on his ankle where the beast had bitten through his army boot, and he still had the memory of the fever, double vision, and excruciating pain he had endured in the hours afterward.

Right now, he had another beast to contend with. The Master of Pain had finished his harira and was paying.

Jacob had made the precaution of paying for his chicken tajine in advance so he could leave at a moment's notice. A pity that would be so soon. It was delicious, and he was only halfway through.

Karim looked away for a moment, so Jacob took the opportunity to glance at his team, a pair of Moroccan state security agents.

The senior agent, Farid, sat at another food stall on the opposite side of Karim, dressed like a businessman and nursing a tea.

Beyond the stalls, near the entrance to the lane into the medina they thought Karim might take, stood Ghanem, dressed in the traditional hooded, brown robe but looking anything but traditional by being draped with gaudy necklaces of plastic beads and fake silver and carrying a basket full of little leather camels. A longtime undercover man, Ghanem had picked props that were so cheap, so ugly, that not even the most clueless tourist would consider buying one. That way he wouldn't be bothered by innocent bystanders in case he had to make a move.

People did take his picture, though. He looked laughable. In a fight, he was anything but.

Karim got up. Jacob bent over his plate and took another forkful of tajine. A Moroccan would have used a piece of bread to scoop some of the food up, and so would Jacob, but he had to look like someone who had never been to North Africa before. The Yankees t-shirt and shorts helped with that.

Karim passed behind him, a couple of stalls between them. It looked like he was headed for the lane where they thought he'd go, one that led, after several twists and turns, to the house of a man suspected as being a fighter in the country's outlawed Al Qaeda of the Islamic Magreb.

They'd follow him there and bust them both.

In Jacob's peripheral vision, he saw Farid set down his tea. Ghanem would be keeping an eye on the target until Farid and Jacob could make their move. Ghanem was too gaudily dressed, too noticeable, to lead the tail. Once the tail was underway, he'd duck into a house down one of the alleys used by the local secret police, shuck off the *djellaba* to reveal modern clothes underneath, and catch up.

Jacob had no fear on that score. Both men knew the labyrinthine alleyways of the old city like the back of their hand.

Farid passed him. Jacob took that as his cue to get up and saunter slowly behind Karim.

The terrorist was about twenty yards ahead of him, with Farid about halfway between Jacob and the terrorist. A tight cluster for tailing, and one Jacob wouldn't use in most situations, but the plaza was so packed with people that they needed to keep that close in order not to lose him.

Up ahead, he saw Ghanem move off down the alley where he was going to do his costume change, still holding up his trinkets to every passing foreigner.

Karim entered the lane, a narrow passage between tall buildings of featureless stone pierced only by a few high and shuttered windows. Farid was right behind him, tailing like a pro by letting a couple of people pass ahead of him to act as a screen. Karim had been a leading terrorist for the better part of a decade, so he would be armed and alert. They had been tailing him all day, and Jacob had noticed that while he never made the obvious move of looking over his shoulder, he always took any turn at a sharp angle, allowing his peripheral vision to take in what had, a moment before, been behind him. He also lingered at shop windows, studying the reflection in the glass for any unwanted followers.

As far as Jacob could tell, Karim didn't know they were there. He hoped it would stay that way. He wouldn't want himself or either of his Moroccan colleagues to end up starring in one of the Master of Pain's videos.

Jacob entered the narrow canyon of the lane, the punishing sun replaced with the shady cool of stone walls and flagstones that only felt the touch of sunlight for an hour a day. The alley bent to the right up ahead. Karim was already out of sight, as were the two innocent pedestrians. Farid was just rounding the corner. Jacob increased his pace slightly.

Just then his phone buzzed in his pocket. He had it set so only an emergency from the control center would set it off.

Control already knew they were tailing the target, so if they were calling him, something more important had just come up.

Perfect timing.

He pulled out his phone and slackened his pace.

"Yes?" he said in a low voice, taking a look over his shoulder. An older Moroccan man with a canvas bag of what looked like groceries walked into the alley, approaching him.

"Come back to control. You're needed elsewhere ASAP," said a male voice in English with a Moroccan accent. He didn't know who. He didn't need to know.

"But we're already—"

"The others can handle this. Time is a factor. You're needed now."

"All right."

He turned and put away his phone. The older man with the canvas bag had gained on him and had been looking right at him. Now, he looked at the ground.

Jacob's heart pounded. Was this one of Karim's men? Was someone tailing the tail?

He couldn't leave now, not with the other members of the team in danger. He had to check this guy out first.

Pretending to text, Jacob walked along the side of the alley where the man was carrying his bag. Just as he came up to him, Jacob bumped into him, hitting the bag with his shin. Something hard and heavy inside banged against it and made a clatter.

Jacob feigned a stumble and fell against the man so he couldn't see his arm slip inside the bag and flip aside a cloth covering whatever lay beneath.

A large ceramic dish covered by a peaked ceramic cover. A tajine dish, and judging by the smell coming out of it, it actually contained a tajine.

"Sorry," Jacob said in loud English. "Wasn't looking where I was going."

"No problem, mister," he said in English, then muttered in Arabic. "How are these people so rich when they are so stupid?"

Jacob hurried back to the Jemaa al-Fna, his shin sore from colliding into an innocent civilian's lunch. He cut across the square as fast as he could, alert for signs of pursuit. No one that he could tell, but with hundreds of people in the square and up on the overlooking balconies, who could really tell?

He grabbed a cab at the edge of the square and had it take him across town.

* * *

Jacob had the cab drop him off three blocks from control. He waited until the taxi drove out of sight before walking the rest of the way.

Control for the Moroccan secret service was a café like any other, a grimy front hiding a dark interior with a dozen men sitting at tables talking, smoking, or watching a TV loudly playing a National Geographic documentary about polar bears. The sort of café where a foreigner gets a second look for entering.

No one gave him a second look. Every single man in there was in one of Morocco's many branches of security service, and they all knew him by sight. Some he'd even been in firefights with.

While Jacob felt bad about leaving Farid and Ghanem alone, he didn't blame the men in here for not helping. Some were guarding this place. Some were too well-known to the Islamist underground to join in the hunt. Others had different specialties. The man winning at backgammon in the far corner was a sniper, and the older fellow across from him cursing his luck was an expert at decoding encrypted radio communications. Tailing was a skill, and you couldn't set just anyone on it, not with someone as paranoid and seasoned as Karim ibn Mohammed.

Jacob cut to the far left of the café, out of sight of the narrow front door and passed the bored-looking proprietor who had black belts in six martial arts, and through a heavy wooden door of faded blue paint.

There was a short hallway and a locked metal door. The door was painted with the warning "Electric relay, do not touch" in Arabic and French along with a couple of lightning bolts to push the point home. A low hum from behind it made a convincing sound effect. Jacob couldn't see it, but there was a miniature camera posing as one of the many black stains on the grimy wall.

The lock clicked open.

Beyond the door and the mountain of Moroccan muscle holding it open was a medium-sized office of transparent glass cubicles, each reaching to the ceiling and shut off by a clear door. In each of these cubicles was a desk, and most of them had an agent sitting at them. Some were listening in on radios or acting as dispatch. Others were surfing jihadist webpages and passing decryption software through images of beheadings and car bombs, looking for writing hidden in the code.

All this activity went on in complete silence, at least as seen from the outside. Each cubicle was noise-proofed so that the classified conversation going on at the next desk couldn't be heard by the operative on the phone next to him, or by sensitive microphones at the other end of the phone conversation.

A Moroccan general sat at a larger cubicle at the end. He had never appeared on television, in a country where the government stations were fond of their generals, and yet, he had more medals than any two of his colleagues. None of those medal ceremonies had been public events.

Because his war was the silent war. The cat-and-mouse with Islamist terror cells, whether homegrown or imported from the rougher areas of the Middle East. One by one, he would hunt down their operatives, question them in whatever ways he deemed necessary, and work his relentless way up their chain of command until he snuffed the cell out.

Over the past fifteen years, he'd done that enough times that no one could estimate how many lives he had saved.

His name was General Jaloul Cherkaoui, and under Moroccan law, Jacob would be executed for ever mentioning that name to anyone.

And Washington would let them. General Cherkaoui had saved a lot of American and European lives too.

Jacob walked up to the general's door, accompanied by the guard who had let him in. The guard saluted through the clear glass. Jacob did not. He was CIA, not military.

General Cherkaoui glanced up from an email he was typing on a laptop, continued typing for a moment, then closed the laptop and nodded. The guard opened the door, and Jacob walked in.

Neither man spoke until the door was closed behind him. The only sound was the low whir of the air circulation system.

The general spoke first, in clipped, careful, but perfectly correct English, "You have been reassigned. You need to fly to Asilah in a helicopter that is waiting for you at the airport. At the Asilah airport, a Land Rover will be at your disposal. You will drive to the coordinates I'm giving you and save an archaeologist from an assassination attempt."

Jacob's heart clenched. He knew an archaeologist working near Asilah.

The general continued, "We have it on good authority that a Tunisian mercenary named El Idrissi has been hired to kill Dr. Jana Peters, who is running an excavation there."

The general showed no indication that he knew of Jacob's and Jana's work together thwarting an attempt by a terrorist group to detonate a crude nuclear bomb in the Suez Canal. There was no need for him to know, so he had never been told.

"We received this information from a reliable informant, although the informant did not know the purpose of the hit. We have the usual records on Dr. Peters, but nothing to indicate that she is a security threat."

Good to see the CIA is a tight enough ship that you don't know who her dad was.

Aaron Peters had extracted Jacob out of Afghanistan after Jacob had a mental breakdown, and he nursed him through the slow process of becoming a functional human being, and then a CIA operative.

Sadly, Aaron Peters was gone now. MIA and presumed dead like so many good men.

General Cherkaoui handed him a dossier. "This is all the information we have on Dr. Peters and El Idrissi. You can read them on the helicopter."

"Thank you, general."

"Good luck, Agent Snow."

Jacob was already walking out, a cold sheen of sweat covering his skin and making the air circulation system feel like an Arctic blast.

Jana's in trouble.

All thought of the mission he had been plucked out of vanished. He had a helicopter to catch.

CHAPTER TWO

A field near Asilah, northwestern Morocco
That evening

Dr. Jana Peters looked out one last time over her excavation as the field crew put tarps over the open squares and trenches before calling it a day and heading back to the dig house. The tarps would keep any windblown dirt or leaves from messing up the tidy portions of the excavated Roman villa the square and trenches had revealed, and would also keep the dew off, essential for preserving the delicate mosaic that they had been uncovering all summer.

Jana had missed much of that. Shortly after making the discovery of a large zodiacal mosaic in what they now knew was the triclinium, the dining room of the villa where the family would receive guests, she had been swept up in the most terrifying two weeks of her life.

The most terrifying, and the most rewarding.

She had done things she had never thought she could achieve and had seen things that she would never forget.

But she was trying to put all that behind her. Jacob, that irritating and fascinating man with strange ties to her late father, had told her in no uncertain terms that he would keep her far away from CIA business from now on. It was only a fluke that her expertise had been needed for that mission, and with her own life in danger, it had made sense for her to be on the team.

Now, life had settled down to its previous routine. She walked over to the mosaic to take another look before her graduate students covered it up for the night. On the very first week of the excavation, some two months ago, a test trench had hit the jackpot and uncovered the edge of this elegant work of ancient art. One panel showed a bull, expertly executed with different shades of brown and black tesserae to create shading, and the one next to it showed two young men in tunics standing side by side.

Taurus and Gemini. Expanding the trench out over the course of the ensuing weeks, her team had gradually uncovered the entire floor of the triclinium, its center dominated by a grand circle showing all the constellations of the zodiac. In the center, a brilliant sun shone, which Jana was relieved to see was made with yellow stone and not gold. They had already had trouble with antiquities thieves, and now the local police had posted a guard through the night.

"It sure is beautiful, isn't it?" said a voice beside her.

Brian stood next to her. He was a handsome graduate student who had worked at a different career for a decade before switching to archaeology. He was about her age, bright and well read, and was good company. Athletic and well-groomed, he was good eye candy too.

Brian obviously thought the same of her, although he hadn't tried anything overt yet. She didn't quite know what she thought about that. Disappointed? Relieved? She still hadn't put the turmoil of the Egyptian mission to rest in her head, so getting involved with a graduate student might not be the best idea.

And yet . . .

"It sure is. The best mosaic I've ever seen under excavation," she said for a lack of anything else to say.

"It's a real privilege working on this dig. This is my first overseas. I did a field school in Illinois and a Middle Mississippian village, then ended up assisting at the field school the next three seasons. It's good to work on the Old World stuff."

"Have you made a decision on what you'll do your dissertation on?"

"Well, as I told you, I want to shift to Old World studies. The Native American sites are interesting, but I want to study my own past."

Jana nodded. "I can understand that. When I was an undergraduate and still trying to figure out my specialty, I did a field school in Guatemala where we worked on a Mayan site. We found a long stretch of beautiful, really well-done bas-reliefs. And yet, they were so alien with their snake gods and people sticking thorns through their tongues. Then a few years later, a professor with some connections got me in Lascaux."

Brian turned to her, his face eager. "You've been to Lascaux?"

Jana laughed. "Sorry to make you jealous. Yes, I spent a whole afternoon there. One of the best days of my life. The paintings of the hunters and wildlife are so vivid, and the way they use the natural shape of the cave to flesh them out is creatively brilliant. But the thing that struck me the most was how *familiar* they seemed. With the Mayan site, I needed all the Mayan symbolism explained to me. This is the goddess of rain. This is a priest performing a ceremony. That professor who took me to Lascaux didn't have to explain anything. I could tell which figures were shamans and which figures were dancing or going on a hunt. It was all familiar. And that's when I realized that these hunter-gatherers from almost 20,000 years ago were like us. They *were* us."

Their eyes met, and the excitement in Brian's showed that he understood. So few really did, even among graduate students, but Brian really did have a passion for the past, not just an intellectual interest in it.

Their gaze lingered on each other for a moment.

The *thwap* of a tarp being laid over the mosaic by a pair of undergraduate students broke the spell. Jana cleared her throat and said, "I'm going to take a walk up the hill. I'll catch you later."

She walked off, flushing with embarrassment.

Why hadn't she invited him along? She was in the habit of walking up a rocky hill overlooking the site every evening to watch the last rays of sun touch the distant Atlantic and look out over the rugged landscape as it turned from gold to crimson to pale blue. This nightly ritual, always performed in solitude, calmed her after a long and demanding day better than a cold beer would have.

She could have invited him along. She knew he wanted her to. The last few times she said she was going on her evening walk, he'd given her a hopeful look.

No, more an *expectant* look. After all the subtle flirting, after all the thrilling conversation, after the weeks of the easy familiarity of excavation life, he figured that they should be ready for the next step.

And yet, Brian waited for her to make the next move. Why? Because she was technically his boss, even though he went to a different university than the one she taught at? Or was it because the field season was coming to an end, and he didn't want a long-distance relationship?

She could ask herself those same questions. Jana had been single for a while now. Career and travel had come first, and while there had been a few short-term relationships, no one really promising had come along. No one who really fired her excitement.

Not even Brian.

Handsome, yes. Intelligent, oh yes. But tempting? Only in an abstract way, and only because it had been so long.

You should really stop flirting with him if you're not going to follow through. It isn't fair.

Or you could just have a fling . . .

As physically appealing as that sounded, the idea left her emotionally cold. She didn't want a fling, not really, but Brian lived in another state. A fling was all they could expect. Besides, the dig was wrapping up soon, so a long-distance relationship built on so little time together would be bound to fail.

She thought all this through as she followed a faint goat trail up a rocky incline to the east of the dig site. It grew steeper, the small stones scattered on the slope looser, and she found her mind focusing more on getting a good footing than running through the soliloquy of "to Brian or not to Brian, that is the question" one more time.

That's why she liked this hike. Oddly, a bit of exercise after an exhausting day actually revived her. As she ascended, the landscape stretched out below her. Already, she could see the distant glitter of the Atlantic to the west. More, and rougher, hills stretched to the east. The one she liked to climb was a mere foothill to a larger range. There was a little village to the south—its square, white houses looked like building blocks gleaming in the late sun. Camp was to the north, consisting of an orderly row of tents and a prefab structure to house the lab and store the finds. She could already see smoke rising from the chow tent as Abdel, the dig cook, created something delicious for dinner. Beyond the camp, a gravel road ran a couple of miles, then turned into a paved road, which in turn became a highway several miles later.

She felt grateful that the highway remained out of sight. She liked the feeling of isolation here.

Just as she got to the summit of the hill, a roughly level area the size of a large living room punctuated by jagged rocks, she paused.

Something wasn't right.

She listened, and other than the soft sound of the wind and the distant *clonk clonk* of sheep's bells from some unseen flock, there was nothing.

So, why had she stopped? Why was her gaze darting all around her while goosebumps rose on her sweating flesh?

She didn't know.

Then something made her look down. Something she had seen out of the corner of her eye, something that had impinged itself onto her subconscious, and from there, the mind's natural instinct for survival made it rise to the conscious and force a physical reaction.

She looked down, and in the grit between the rocks, she saw a footprint of a large person wearing boots.

The local shepherds wore sandals. The only people who wore boots locally in this area were military and her own crew, and she knew none of her own crew had been up here, at least not in the past few hours, as the crispness of the boot print would indicate.

When you think you might be hunted, don't act like prey.

That's what her father had told her when they played soldiers in the woods.

Act casual. Unconcerned. But remain alert.

Jana pretended to look out at the view as she always did, but instead of gazing far to the horizon, she lowered her eyes to look at the rocks and declivities nearby. She made a slow turn, ears perked for any noise.

Nothing. She kept turning, intending on making a slow circuit and then leaving. She didn't know if this footprint meant nothing or something very serious, but she'd skip her evening routine today.

She didn't get a chance. Jana had only made it halfway through her circle when, just to her left and at a spot she would have examined in the next second, she heard a slight sound of movement.

She whirled to face it, and saw a North African man, young and wide-shouldered, dressed in boots, jeans, and a loose shirt, studying her with narrowed eyes.

Jana didn't see any more of his features. She couldn't keep her eyes off the pistol in his hand.

"Don't move," he ordered in Arabic. "And don't pretend you don't understand me."

He spoke with a Tunisian accent.

Slowly, Jana raised her hands halfway up, still close to her center so she could use them to block or strike. Her father had taught her these things, too, although she was long out of practice. He'd gone MIA years ago.

The man paced forward.

"What do you want?" Jana asked. The evenness of her tone surprised her.

The Tunisian didn't reply. As he approached, he reached his free hand into his pocket and came out with a flex cuff, basically a giant plastic zip tie like many police officers use instead of the old-style metal handcuffs.

"Turn around and put your hands behind your back."

Not going to happen.

She waited until he was in reach. He gestured with his gun and opened his mouth, probably to repeat the order, when Jana brought her left hand slamming down on his wrist and her right hand in a vicious jab for his Adam's apple.

At least that's what she tried to do.

The Tunisian moved his gun hand forward, so her blow landed on the rock-hard muscles of his forearm rather than the more vulnerable area of his wrist. At the same time, he brought up his free hand to block her punch, slamming her arm aside with such force that Jana staggered.

The Tunisian gave her a front kick to her stomach that left her doubled over and coughing on the ground.

"That's more like it," the Tunisian said. "Now, I'm going to put these cuffs on and then I have to make a little video. My clients requested it as part of the job."

CHAPTER THREE

Jacob scrambled up the hill, hoping he wasn't too late. He'd been stalking the Tunisian mercenary El Idrissi for the better part of two hours as the guy took a back route to get to a hill overlooking Jana's dig camp. This move had confused him. While he had allowed the Tunisian to stay well ahead of him to reduce the chances of being spotted, Jacob could see that he didn't have a sniper's rifle. So, he wasn't going to pick off Jana at long distance. Observe the camp for a while before slipping in at night? That seemed more likely, although there was another hill just to the east of camp that would make a better vantage point.

Intrigued and worried, Jacob had watched his quarry get close to the top of the hill before getting on his belly and worming his way through the rough terrain.

Jacob only caught glimpses of him after that.

Then when Jacob had gotten two-thirds of the way up the hill, he heard the sound of footsteps ahead and to his left.

Jana walked into view.

Damn it, this is probably some daily routine, and the people who hired this guy knew it.

Jacob resisted the urge to shout a warning. That might invite a shot. Perhaps El Idrissi was hired to kidnap her or question her.

He hoped so, because if he was going to just kill her at the first opportunity, there was no way Jacob was going to get up there in time.

Still, he moved up, keeping low, trying to stick to cover while trying to keep quiet.

An almost impossible task. Every few steps, a little noise from the loose ground would betray him.

Hopefully, El Idrissi was so focused on Jana, who had disappeared beyond the brow of the hill, that he wouldn't notice his approach. Sweat slicked the grip of Jacob's automatic pistol, but his hand remained steady.

He heard voices, a man's and then Jana's familiar tones. He felt a sudden surge of desire and tamped it down. Now wasn't the time.

Never was the time with that woman, for all sorts of reasons.

He heard the sound of a struggle. Jacob increased his pace.

As he got close to the brow of the hill, he went on his belly and wormed his way between the rocks. A narrow gully to his right, about the width and depth of a bathtub, offered him a way up that would conceal him completely, but the countless little rocks in it would shift and betray him.

Surprise was key. El Idrissi hadn't simply shot her as soon as she appeared, so he wanted to keep her alive for a while at least. That gave Jacob time to get into position. He hoped.

He stuck to more solid ground, eyes constantly roving, looking for the Tunisian.

Jacob found Jana first, lying on her side on the fairly flat top of the hill, doubled over and coughing. His heart clenched, and a cold, sick fear washed over him at the sight of such a strong woman reduced to something so helpless.

Her hands were behind her back, and while Jacob couldn't see them, they looked under constraint.

What he didn't see was her attacker.

Jana looked up and around, then shouted, "He hid to my rear left."

She said this in Arabic, thinking whoever had spooked the Tunisian was a local.

Boy, is she going to be surprised.

Assuming we both live through the next ten seconds.

He didn't see anything where Jana indicated, and he was well hidden enough, peeking through a shadowed crevice between two stones with a bush behind him to cut his profile, that Jana didn't see him.

So, where the hell was the Tunisian? El Idrissi must have heard Jacob coming up the mountain and hid. If he had any sense of the direction Jacob had approached from, then he'd circle around the hill and come at Jacob from Jacob's right.

The hiss of several small stones being displaced told him that the Tunisian was coming for him faster than he anticipated.

El Idrissi had come through the gully, the same gully Jacob had skipped.

Jacob hunkered down but didn't hear the sound repeat. El Idrissi had traversed it. He wasn't going up or down.

That meant he was close. Close enough that a gunfight might end up being fatal for the both of them.

Why aren't grenades standard issue in the CIA?

Jacob decided to risk it all on a sudden appearance. Making his best guess as to his silent opponent's location, he popped up from behind the rock to his right, leveling his gun.

He had misjudged by a hair. Swiveling his gun to where he saw the Tunisian's half-concealed form, he let off a shot just as the Tunisian fired too.

The Tunisian's bullet cracked off a rock just by Jacob's leg and then the mercenary dropped out of sight.

Jacob shifted to a more covered position but couldn't find anything too good because the man was downslope from him. He kept his gun trained on where El Idrissi had disappeared, waiting for him to reveal himself, straining past the ringing in his ears for any sound of movement.

The man's arm appeared. Jacob fired, and the arm dropped out of sight. A grenade sketched a perfect parabola with himself at its end.

Jacob had no place to hide, and no time to hide there.

Jacob leapt up and swatted the grenade as if he was playing badminton and his hand was the racquet. The heavy steel globe stung his palm, but his move had the effect of sending the grenade back down the slope.

Jacob hit the dirt just as it went off in a plume of dust and a patter of falling stones.

He saw flailing through the cloud. Squinting, it took him a second to figure out what he was seeing. The grenade had dislodged a large rock and several smaller ones just above the Tunisian's hiding place, setting off a minor avalanche that the mercenary got caught in. Jacob got a brief glimpse of him staggering out from the onslaught, battered and bleeding, before the dust obscured him again.

Jacob fired all ten remaining rounds from his magazine in a low fan pattern all around where the guy could be hiding.

The dust began to clear. Jacob got to one knee and snapped another clip in the pistol.

The dust cleared more, blowing up above the hillside like an expanding wraith. El Idrissi lay sprawled on his back, his pistol out of reach, and his mouth open, gasping. He had a widening bloodstain on his shirt, one on his shoulder, and another on his thigh.

The chest shot was the one that counted. Even from a distance and through ears ringing from the gunshots and explosion, he could hear the telltale bubbling wheeze of a punctured lung. The man was hemorrhaging blood both internally and externally.

"You OK, Jana?"

"Yeah."

"Are there any more?" he asked, looking around. He hadn't seen any while stalking the Tunisian, but it paid to be careful.

"No."

"Hold on."

"Untie me!"

"Hold on."

Jacob moved with care down to the mercenary, keeping low and keeping a sharp eye on the dying man. He may have been plugged three times, but that didn't meant he was down for the count.

As he approached, the Tunisian flailed his arms a bit, trying to sit or move or draw a weapon. Jacob wasn't sure. His movements were too weak, too uncoordinated.

Unless it was a trick.

It was.

With a speed remarkable for one so injured, the mercenary reached under his leg, pulled out a knife hidden there, and threw it straight at Jacob's throat.

It would have skewered Jacob's Adam's apple if he had been a little quicker and a little less injured. Instead, Jacob nailed El Idrissi right between the eyes just as he was about to release. The hand twitched, and the knife hissed past his ear.

Damn it, I wanted to question him!

Jacob shrugged it off. El Idrissi had been a pro. He doubted the guy would have told him anything.

He approached, studying the body to make sure El Idrissi hadn't set up any death switch or movement trigger. Wouldn't want to start searching this asshole and have him go off like the Fourth of July.

Jacob couldn't see any wires or triggers. Probably wouldn't have had time to set one up anyway. His last trick was concealing that knife and acting like he was dying.

The acting job had been the easy part. Jacob could have sat out of reach for ten minutes, and it would have all been over, but he had questions, questions that now wouldn't get answered.

Like who wanted to go after Jana, and why.

"Hey, Jacob, get your ass over here and untie me!"

"Hold on."

"Hold on? I'm trussed up like a Thanksgiving turkey here."

"I said hold on," Jacob replied, annoyed.

He searched the body. Besides a couple of spare clips, a wallet with an ID with the right picture and the wrong name, and a thousand dollars-worth of Moroccan dirhams, all he found was a phone. Locked with a code, of course. He knew someone back in that café in Marrakech who could break into this easily enough, assuming he was going back to Marrakech. He couldn't say why, but he smelled another long mission coming up.

He took out his own phone and took a photo of the body's bloodied face, then of a mole on the left hand that would be a distinguishing mark. The same for a scar on the right hand.

Back in Afghanistan, there had been guys who took photos of their kills as a sort of trophy. Jacob had never done that. This was for the record, to send to the Moroccans and all other allied governments so they knew there was one less scumbag in the world.

"What the hell? Are you taking photos of a dead body?"

Jana had made it to her feet and stood, arms bound behind her back, at the top of the hill looking down at him.

"Proof of death," Jacob said, walking up the slope toward her. "It's not like I'm going to print it into a poster or anything."

"Good to hear."

Her voice wavered a little, the joking barely covering up the shock of what had just happened. She was cool in a fight, but the aftershock always hit her hard. It hit Jacob Snow hard, too, once upon a time.

"What did he say to you?" Jacob asked as he came up to her and pulled out a Bowie knife. Jana turned around so he could cut her bonds.

"Nothing, other than he was going to make a video before . . ." Jana let out a little shudder and Jacob almost sliced her hand.

He held her hands in his. "Hold still," he said in a gentle tone.

Jana took a deep breath. Her shoulders relaxed a little. The trembling continued. Jacob squeezed her hands, and they finally became still.

He cut through the binding plastic. She rubbed her wrists and turned to him.

"Thank you. What the hell's going on?"

"No idea. Just got some intel that someone hired this guy to take out a hit on you. The CIA sent me to intercept."

"All the way from Greece?"

Greece was where Jacob was based and where he had his home, on the rare occasions he got to stay there.

"No. I was . . . closer."

"Thank you."

Their gaze held for a second. Jana looked away first, out over the distant camp. A crowd of archaeologists and students, barely bigger than dots, stood outside the chow tent. Another group was making its way toward the hill. Jacob caught the blue uniform of the police officer he'd been told was on duty.

"They'll be here in twenty minutes." Jana told him. She turned to him and found him lying pone, peeking over a rock.

"Go down and meet them," he said. "Say you heard a gunfight up here and ran. You didn't see anything. I'll cut out in the other direction."

He took a step away, unsure how to say goodbye. It was great to see her again, even given the circumstances, but this was no social call, and he needed to get going. He nodded to her and turned away.

"But wait, what the hell is happening?" She called out after him.

He found himself walking back to her. "I'm sorry, but I don't know. We'll dig into this. In the meantime, keep vigilant."

Jacob was about to turn away a second time when his phone buzzed. Why the hell did something important always come up when he was already in the middle of something important?

He turned up the sound as he answered to hear over the ringing of his ears.

To his surprise, his boss, Tyler Wallace at the CIA station in Athens, was on the other end of the secured line.

"Snow, you finish the job?"

"Just did. Target is neutralized, and his target is safe. I was just about to hide. Witnesses on their way."

Jacob wondered why Wallace didn't simply wait until he checked in with a status report like he always did.

He got his answer a moment later. "Good job, Snow. Now get back to Asilah airport ASAP. Take the helicopter to Tangier, where you'll be flown to Durham in northern England."

"Wait. Jana might still be in danger. If they sent one guy, they could send another."

"Local operatives will watch over the dig site."

Jacob glanced at the archaeologist. "That might not be—"

"You have your orders, agent. The general is sending a couple of good men up. They'll be there within the hour."

"But maybe I should—"

"Get going, agent." Wallace was beginning to sound irritated. Not a good thing with a man like that.

"So, what's going on?"

"You need to investigate the murder of a certain Professor Arnold Woburn. We'll send you the dossier. We've picked up some chatter that he was murdered by a terror cell planning operations in the Middle East."

Jacob nodded. That region was his specialty. He hardly ever got called as far north as England unless it was directly related to events down here.

"Will do." He hung up.

He turned to Jana and realized he had a far bigger problem.

She was looking at him, eyes wide with concern.

"Professor Woburn was killed? I knew him!"

Jacob grimaced. He had screwed up. He'd turned up the phone to get above the ringing in his ears, forgetting that Jana was close by and hadn't been firing a weapon. She overheard everything.

"That was a classified call. Pretend you didn't hear it."

Jana stepped forward. "Do you need my help?"

"No." He made the reply as curt as possible to discourage her from asking any more questions. Then he turned and ran off. He needed to get as much distance between himself and that archaeological field crew as possible.

And get plenty of distance between himself and Jana Peters.

No, Jana, I probably don't need your help, but I sure want it.

CHAPTER FOUR

Durham University, England
8 a.m. The next day

"It's so terrible," the university chancellor said. "The police say there's no sign of robbery. Could it have been some sort of personal vendetta? It's hard to imagine. He was so quiet and studious."

"We haven't eliminated any possibilities," Jacob said.

True enough. The chatter that Wallace had spoken about was vague, only that Woburn had been taken out by a terror cell that was planning operations somewhere in the Middle East. Jacob wasn't even privy to the source or sources of this information. So often, it was some intermediary, some fixer or arms dealer, who made money on the side and bought protection by feeding choice bits of information to the CIA.

So, one or more of these individuals had had dealings with this group and knew of or guessed at their involvement in the Woburn murder. The fact that the source or sources didn't reveal the name of the group showed that they were afraid. And CIA informants are generally not the kind of people who get easily spooked.

So, whoever did this was pretty damn scary.

He was being led to the history department by the nervous-looking chancellor, a portly man with a big bald patch and the stain of a hastily eaten breakfast on the lapel of his sports coat. Jacob had presented himself, with a little help from the embassy in London, as an FBI agent. Woburn had been an American citizen, and thus the embassy was expected to send up personnel.

Durham was a prestigious university in a small town in northern England. Most of the university stood on a high hill overlooking town. The impressive effect was heightened by the fact that rolling plains surrounded Durham, making the eminence visible for miles around. A famous cathedral with a soaring steeple stood on one side of the hilltop, and the university quad was surrounded by imposing stone buildings with crenellation on the roof to look like a castle. At this hour, it was fairly quiet, just some groundskeepers and a few early risers.

Jacob wasn't sure what he was looking for. He had already seen Professor Woburn's body at the local morgue. The professor had been found in a field, beaten and then garroted. All identifying papers were missing, not that that slowed down identification for long. His wife had already reported him missing the previous night.

His car had been found by the side of the road. No signs of struggle. His laptop and some school papers still inside.

"His office is in here, in the history department," the chancellor indicated a Victorian building up ahead.

They passed through a heavy wooden door, and Jacob found himself in a large dining hall, tables and chairs set for at least a couple of hundred students and faculty. An arcade ran around the upper story, and there Jacob could see breastplates, helmets, and buff coats dating to the English Civil war, along with swords, muskets, and lances. There were also various oil portraits of historic figures.

No one else was in the room, and it felt more like a museum as their footsteps echoed back at them from the rafters.

They passed through another door at the far end and up some stairs, the chancellor huffing and gripping the rail. Jacob felt tempted to take him to the gym. This guy couldn't have been more than in his mid-fifties, and already his body was conking out on him.

They got to the top, the chancellor taking a moment to catch his breath, and then passed down a hall to an office that the chancellor opened with a key.

"We kept it locked in anticipation of your arrival."

"Thank you."

Jacob saw a standard academic office—desk, bookshelves, and a computer. The local police had already gone through his email and found nothing of use. He hadn't chatted with whomever killed him via email, and the guy was too old for social media. He didn't have accounts on any of the platforms.

Jacob checked the desk drawers but, as he expected, didn't find anything. Then he turned to the bookshelves, which for an individual like this was usually the key. When someone spends their life buried in books, checking out the titles is like reading their autobiography.

He found books in English, Greek, and Hebrew.

"A lot of books in Hebrew," Jacob noted. "All Biblical studies or archaeology."

"You speak Hebrew?" the chancellor said, standing at the doorway.

"A little."

Enough to work with a squad of Israeli commandoes to take out a terrorist bomb-making workshop. Ah, good times!

"Although he was fascinated by Jewish history, especially Biblical history, Professor Woburn wasn't Jewish. He was rather unusual in the field for being an agnostic with no Jewish heritage. I don't think antisemitism was the motive," the chancellor looked at him and then added quickly, "Although you're better qualified to make that call."

Jacob suppressed a smile. *So, you're assuming I'm Jewish? The Israeli commandos knew better. But it brings up an interesting point—how many of my enemies of the bearded type think I'm a Jew?*

I guess it doesn't matter. After all I've done to them, they'd kill me slow no matter what my faith.

He scanned some of the volumes for Woburn's name on the spine before discovering all his works sat on a single shelf, no matter what their topic or language. A man proud of his accomplishments, which at least in word count was impressive. Jacob counted ten books by him alone, with at least another thirty with him as coauthor or editor.

"He was pretty prominent?"

"A leading scholar and a field worker who was much in demand, although he quit archaeology a few years ago."

"Really?" Jacob turned to him. "Why?"

"He was frustrated that the Israeli government interfered with an excavation he was on. So, he focused on history instead."

"Interfered? How?"

The chancellor looked confused. "Well, I can't really say. He didn't speak much about it, only that his team discovered old papyri preserved in a sealed pot at Tel Shimon, much like the Dead Sea Scrolls in the Qumran caves. They dated to the Bar Kokhba revolt in the second century AD, the third Jewish revolt against Roman rule. Some fascinating material on battles we hadn't even heard of, as well as information on the day-to-day religious worship of the time. While he never came out and said it, Woburn made it known to me and several of our colleagues that he was very upset that the Israeli government didn't allow his translations of some of the papyri to be published. In fact, they confiscated them."

"Why would they do that?"

"Well, I'm not a specialist in that area, my focus is on Ottoman diplomatic history, I was Professor of Political Science before taking my current position, but from what I've heard from Professor Woburn and others, the Israeli government is very particular about what ancient documents get published. They want to, um, control the narrative."

"Control the narrative?" Jacob was still rifling through the books while keeping a sharp focus on what the man was saying.

"Israel was born out of a long desire for a Jewish homeland, and after the Holocaust, the Zionists decided enough was enough and began an armed struggle against British colonial forces. They also fought the Palestinians, who had their own independence struggle against the British. Eventually, in 1948, Israel became a nation. Jews flooded in from all over the world, especially Europe. Israel is even more of a nation of immigrants than your own country. The nation's leaders had to build a country from scratch. They developed modern Hebrew, essentially a constructed language with elements of ancient Hebrew and Yiddish that everyone could learn. They also had to forge a national identity, not just as Jews but as Israelis. So, they looked to the past, the Temple period and the fights against the Romans and the Canaanites and all the other rival powers."

"And what does this have to do with Woburn's excavation?" Jacob asked, flipping through one of the archaeological field reports for Tel Shimon. Like a lot of university professors, this guy took his time getting to the point.

"In order to create a national identity, a nation must have a set narrative, something everyone agrees on. Take your own American Revolution, for example. All the colonists rose up against the unfair taxes of King George III, united in a desire for freedom. In fact, only about a third of the people in the thirteen colonies actively supported the Revolution. Another third were the so-called Tories, who supported the Crown. Many signed up for the British army or fled to Canada. The remaining third were neutral. This gets glossed over in history books because it hurts the narrative. Americans want to believe they were a united nation from the start. Good guys versus bad guys. It's normal in all nations, especially such a young and troubled nation as Israel."

"And Woburn's excavation?" Jacob found the section for important finds and began skimming through it. While his Hebrew was only mediocre, he hoped it would be good enough to find what he was looking for.

"It isn't the first time the Israelis have suppressed or channeled information. It was years before they allowed a translation of the Dead Sea Scrolls. They wanted to make sure the translation fit with the national construct of their ancient past. Also, ancient texts that show things embarrassing to their history, such as Jews who collaborated with the Romans or criticisms of the great national heroes, are often suppressed."

"Did Woburn mention what was in the suppressed papyri?"

"No, he didn't. Apparently, he was told in no uncertain terms that if he spoke about it, he could forget ever excavating Israeli sites or using Israeli archives."

"Do you know anyone who might know more?"

"The other people on the excavation, but they're all Israeli. I don't think you'll get them to talk."

"Did he have an assistant? A grad student or something who helps with the translations?"

"Yes. A young Israeli student, I believe. I recall Woburn being quite upset when he was killed in a car crash."

Interesting.

Then Jacob found something even more interesting.

A series of photographs of a sealed clay jar. The photos showed it being excavated, and then opened, showing a packet of papyri still wrapped with a leather strap after all those years.

Jacob puzzled through the Hebrew. While he didn't understand a lot of the technical terms—he doubted he would have understood them in English either—he did get the gist of it. The jar contained a packet of letters and historical documents dating from the Bar Kokhba rebellion against the Romans from 132 to 135 AD. The initial assessment was that they were military correspondence and accounts of religious worship. A note at the end of the section said, "full translation in volume two."

Jacob grabbed volume two of the excavation report off the shelf, saw a volume three, and grabbed that too.

"I'm going to need to take these as evidence."

The chancellor looked uncertain. "Oh! Um, well—"

"Thank you for your help."

Jacob walked out the door, the chancellor having to scurry to get out of the way.

Jacob hadn't found out much, only a thread to pull on.

Arnold Woburn had found something in that jar that the Israelis didn't want published, something that changed history, or revealed too much about it. Woburn had been furious at having that document suppressed but had swallowed his pride for the sake of his career.

Then someone had come after him years later.

Were those two events related? Maybe. Probably. But who would want to ice him?

Not Mossad. Not in this clumsy of a fashion. Woburn had been beaten to a pulp before being finished off, and his car had simply been left on the side of the road for anyone to discover. The Israeli secret service would have fixed his car to make him crash or dosed his drink with untraceable chemicals that would have given him a heart attack.

So not Mossad. But who else would have known about the contents of the jar? Did other elements of the Israeli government do this for their own factional reasons? Someone else on the dig, perhaps?

And then there was that graduate student who died in a car crash. The excavation report had a full list of the crew. Jacob would send that to the researchers at the CIA so they could correlate that with newspaper reports of car crashes in Israel. They'd find out who it was. That would be another thread of investigation because Jacob didn't believe for a minute that that car accident was actually an accident.

He could chase that information himself, of course, but he'd leave it to the backup team. He had other things to do.

Like get down to London as quickly as possible. There was a place there where he could ask questions and maybe find some answers.

Assuming he didn't get knifed just for showing up.

CHAPTER FIVE

The Negev Desert in southern Israel is one of the most desolate spots in a region full of desolate spots. A wasteland of rocky hills separated by broad stretches of desert, little grows here except a few scraggly bushes on shaded hillsides and clusters of palms and acacia in the rare oasis or wadi. Here and there people have dug wells deep into the rock to create a patch of green in the background brown, a haven of life in a relentless landscape of thirst and lack.

And yet, this was one of the most active regions in all of Israel. Wedged as it was between the Red Sea, Jordan, and with easy sailing to Egypt, it was rife with smugglers.

To be a smuggler in the Negev was to be a Negev Bedouin, one of the several tribes who had wandered this land with their flocks for centuries. Knowing no government, caring little who was in charge, and paying even less attention to official decrees, the Bedouin felt they could do what they wanted in their territory.

And what they wanted was to make as much money as possible smuggling goods across international borders.

Because what was a border but an imaginary line in the ground between land ruled by one group of rich city dwellers and another group of rich city dwellers?

Rich, but out of touch. These borders weren't wells or patches of forage for animals. Not anything real. They were lines on a map in the capital. In the far east of the Negev where the River Jordan provided a miracle of water, the border ran right down the middle of the river! If the Israelis were as strong as they said they were, they would have taken the entire river from the Jordanians. If the dissolute city Muslims in Amman were really as devout as they said they were, Allah would have allowed them to take the entire river for themselves.

It didn't matter. Let the city dwellers draw their lines on paper. It only provided opportunity for profit.

Carl Bryson, an American outdoorsman who had worked every job from safari trip leader to deep sea fisherman, was not a Negev Bedouin. He was from a place as unlike the Negev as any place on earth—New Jersey. But he had lived with the Beni Nimir tribe for two years, learned their language and their ways, and taught them a great deal as well. He had earned their respect with his hardiness in the desert and his deadly accuracy with a rifle. They had earned his respect with their deep knowledge of the land and a fierce independence that would put even the staunchest American Libertarian to shame.

So, it was with great pleasure that Carl Bryson sat in a black, goat's hair tent with two of his assistants facing Sheikh Abdelrahman ibn Rahim, the sheikh's two grown sons, three of his brothers, and one of their cousins.

There were, of course, no women in the tent. A couple of boys had brought the platters of food, jugs of water, and goat's milk from the women's tent. The boys had lingered at the tent opening to stare at the foreigners before the sheikh shooed them away.

"It is an honor to sit in your tent, Sheikh Abdelrahman ibn Rahim," Carl Bryson said, taking another handful of succulent goat's meat and popping it into his mouth.

"And an honor to have you with us again, Mr. Bryson," the sheikh said, grabbing a fine morsel and putting it on Bryson's side of the platter. Bryson picked it up and ate it to acknowledge the sheikh's hospitality.

"I am afraid that I am going to have to be rude and start discussing business before we have finished eating," Bryson said.

The sheikh shook his head. "Business before tea—"

"Causes stomach cramps. When food is before you, business can wait," Bryson interrupted.

The sheikh smiled. "You have remembered our sayings."

"You taught me well."

"We never taught you how to live at a proper pace in life. Always in a hurry. But I suppose you have your reasons. To answer the question you will ask next, Mr. Bryson, yes, we did get the ANFO. Two hundred kilos of it."

"Good. That's good."

ANFO, ammonium nitrate and fuel oil, was a common blasting agent used in mining. Pound for pound, it was as powerful as dynamite and much more stable. It could handle rough transport across open desert. Two hundred kilos were well more than they needed, not that Bryson was going to complain. You could really never have too many explosives, as Gerald Hunter, the explosives expert sitting to his right, had said many times.

One of the sheikh's sons pulled up a tarp near the back of the tent to reveal a stack of heavy plastic bags marked ANFO in Hebrew and English. He hauled one over and slit it open with a curved knife hanging from his belt.

Hunter held out a hand and the Bedouin poured a heap of little pink beads into it. Hunter examined them for a moment, sniffed them, and nodded to Bryson. He then poured his handful of ammonium nitrate and fuel oil back into the bag, and the young Bedouin used some duct tape to seal it up.

"So, a thousand dollars per kilo, as we agreed?" Bryson asked.

"Yes, that will be acceptable," the sheikh replied.

Ten times the market price, but regular citizens couldn't buy ANFO, certainly not in Israel. The sheikh must have stolen it from one of Negev's mining operations or bought it from an employee who had.

Brett Fisher, the man to his left, pulled out a wad of hundred-dollar bills and stacked them up. One of the sheikh's brothers pulled out a battery-operated money counting machine and fed the hundreds through. The whir of the electric device sounded surreal in a tent adorned with rugs and swords that would not have looked out of place a thousand years ago.

The brother nodded and tucked the hefty stack of notes inside his robes.

"I'm glad that went well for both of us," the sheikh said. "Eat, my friends. It is too long since you have had proper desert food."

"Oh, but sheikh, I have some gifts for you," Bryson said, patting a duffel bag by his side. A duffel bag that, given his position of trust in the tribe, hadn't been searched by the Bedouin when they arrived.

"That is most kind of you, my friend." The sheikh's eyes sparkled with interest. Bryson's gifts had always been good ones.

Bryson unzipped the duffel bag. No one kept a close eye on him. He was too well-known. Too well trusted.

"Firstly, a collection of fine perfumes from Paris to delight your nostrils when you visit the women's tent."

The unmarried younger men laughed nervously, elbowed each other, and whispered dirty comments.

Bryson handed over several ornate bottles.

"Next, a pair of high-powered handheld radios. Better for communication than cell phones, which have poor coverage here—as you know—and can be traced."

He handed over the radios. They earned more interest than the perfume. The Bedouin were a practical lot. Living in such conditions, they had to be.

"And finally . . ." Bryson paused, searching his heart for feelings, and only finding determination. ". . . a Scorpion EVO 3 submachine gun with a hundred-round drum magazine and altered to fire at full auto."

He pulled the Czech-made machine gun out of his duffel bag, flicked off the safety, and sprayed the closely packed Bedouins sitting at point-blank range in front of him.

The nomads screamed and flailed. To either side of Bryson, his companions pulled out pistols and added to the fire. A couple of Bedouins managed to draw their own weapons, but never got to use them before bullets tore through their bodies.

Within seconds, they were all dead.

But the firing did not stop. It was all over the camp now, as Bryson's other men took out the rest of the camp—the men who had stood sentry watching for Israeli patrols, the women and girls who had cooked dinner, and the boys who had served it.

Bryson and his companions double tapped the Bedouins in the tent, then rushed out to help with the fight.

But it was already over. Half a dozen of his men were finishing off the last of the wounded, cursing and raging as they did so.

A moment later, Bryson saw the reason for their anger. Smith lay dead with a gunshot between the eyes. Didier lay gasping and thrashing in the sand, shot in the gut.

"Damn it, I told you to be careful with the sentries. These guys are good!" Bryson raged. He couldn't afford to lose men, not before the big operation.

"Sorry, sir," one of the survivors said. "They were so quick."

"Like I told you! What did I tell you?"

"Inferior races are still dangerous races," the man repeated the phrase Bryson had drilled into them over and over again.

Bryson jerked a thumb toward the tent. "Go in there, get the explosives, and load them into the backs of the Jeeps. Fisher, retrieve those radios. We'll need them. And get our money back if it isn't too bloody."

The men hurried to do what they were told.

Bryson walked over to Didier as he writhed in the sand. A good fighter. Ex-French Foreign Legion. It was a shame that they couldn't take him along.

Didier looked up at him with eyes that had trouble focusing. Bryson saw disappointment there, and frustration, but no fear. Not with someone like Didier.

"You know the agreement," Bryson said. "We don't have time for wounded. The mission is too important."

"H . . . help me stand," Didier said, his heavy accent and halting breath making the words almost incomprehensible. "I . . . I want to die standing."

Bryson slung his machine gun over his shoulder, knelt down, and draped one of the Frenchman's arms over his shoulder. Then he lifted him up. Didier cried out in pain, knees buckling, and Bryson struggled under the man's full weight. He carried him a few steps before Didier got his legs working and, gasping and leaking blood down Bryson's trouser leg, made it to the nearest tent, where he leaned heavily against a pole. Bryson made sure he was standing on his own and backed off.

Didier tried to stand a little straighter, composing himself.

Bryson unslung his machine gun and leveled it at him. "I'm sorry you didn't get to see it, my friend."

The Frenchman snapped out his right arm in a Fascist salute.

"Heil Hitler!" he cried.

Bryson gave him a burst to the head.

CHAPTER SIX

Trains are slow and inefficient in the UK, and so despite leaving Durham in the early afternoon, Jacob Snow didn't make it down to London until evening.

That suited him fine. It gave him time to puzzle through the archaeological report and hear back from the research guys in the CIA that the crewmember who died in a car crash was Mosche Cohen, a graduate student studying ancient languages at Hebrew University in Jerusalem. The chancellor had the date wrong. In fact, Cohen had died the previous year, only ten months ago.

The narrow gap of time made this accident seem even less like a coincidence.

While the CIA didn't have access to the police reports, newspaper accounts said that Cohen had been driving through a mountainous region at night when he swerved suddenly off the road, broke through a barrier, and rolled down into a ravine.

Standard hit. Have a watcher radio ahead when the target drives past, then up the road is the other half of the team, a guy in a big truck who times it so that he comes on the target at a sharp bend. The truck swerves into the target's lane, the target panics, and boom. Game over.

Jacob spent the rest of the journey reading through three volumes of archaeology in Hebrew. It gave him a headache, and he wished Jana Peters was there to take this part of the job. She'd read through it quicker and get more out of it.

But she wasn't there, and she wasn't going to be. It was bad enough that he lost Aaron Peters, his mentor and savior. He wasn't about to lose the man's daughter too.

The field report talked about excavations at Tel Shimon. A *tel* was an artificial hill created by centuries of human habitation. People living on the same spot would build atop previous foundations, fill in cellars in order to have more ground space, and cover up refuse pits with fresh soil. All of these actions over the centuries would slowly raise the ground level and after enough time, the current town would be atop a hill made entirely of the remains of previous settlements. Tels were found all across the Middle East and were a treasure trove for archaeologists.

Tel Shimon near the River Jordan in eastern Israel was special for a couple of reasons. Although inhabited since the Neolithic, it had never been a major center for trade or political power, and yet, it was still inhabited when Bar Kokhba started his revolt. Local legend had that it was here that he gave a speech that rallied thousands of troops to his cause, bringing the entire region into revolt against the hated Romans. Thus, the place became known as Tel Shimon, after Bar Kokhba's first name Shimon.

Jacob looked up the meaning of the name and found it meant "one who has heard." Perhaps because he heard the call of God to rebel? Bar Kokhba meant "son of the star" in Aramaic, another language used frequently by Jews at the time, and referred to something called the Star Prophecy. This was a verse from Numbers 24:17: "There shall come a star out of Jacob," which was interpreted by some rabbis as a prediction of a coming messiah.

Shimon Bar Kokhba's followers certainly believed that and fought with tenacity against the local Roman legions for three long years. For a time, Bar Kokhba carved out his own state and issued coinage, but once the full weight of the Roman Empire turned against the Jews, they didn't have a chance. The rebellion was crushed, its leaders executed, and the Jews scattered or were sold into slavery. Tel Shimon was burnt to the ground and remained unoccupied for three hundred years until a small Byzantine town was founded there.

All of this was in the report. What wasn't in the report was what had been in the damn jar that had been so important that the Israeli government suppressed it. Woburn hadn't even put any notes in the margins to give Jacob a clue.

There was a hint in the text, however, something the censors missed.

In the introduction to volume two, the volume devoted to translations of the papyri, Woburn mentioned that the documents "discussed the preservation and protection of Jewish holy objects." But when Jacob read through the translations, he found nothing of the kind. There was a specific papyrus that discussed who should replace a couple of rabbis killed in a Roman massacre. Another document was a request for four different plants needed for the celebration of the feast of Sukkot. There was also a bundle of letters between one of Bar Kokhba's generals and a rabbi about how to present the rebel leader as a messiah. The rabbi's flock had many doubters, and the rabbi and the general talked about how to bring these people around.

All interesting stuff, but nothing about preserving Jewish artifacts from Roman pillage.

That must have been the document the Israelis barred from publication.

But why?

He didn't know anyone down in London who he could ask, but he did know a place where he could ask around for information on hits in the UK. In fact, it was the same place where a lot of those hits were planned, and a hitman was hired.

The train pulled into King's Cross station in central London as the sky turned from the deep blue of dusk to black. The Two Duelists would just be getting into a swinging night.

The Two Duelists was a pub near Elephant and Castle on the south bank of the Thames. It had the reputation of being a dangerous boozer, but only to the civilians. Those in the know knew it to be a center of information and illegal deals.

Jacob had known a place like that in Beirut—Hassan's basement bar. The bar wasn't actually called that, he wasn't sure if it even had a name, and he was pretty sure it wasn't licensed as a business, but that was what everyone called it. A great place to listen to the pulse of the Middle East. Too bad that the last time he went there a Kyrgyz killer-for-hire named Chingis Beshimov exposed him as CIA, which nearly got him killed.

And Jana. She'd been tagging along. It was amazing how much he'd been thinking about her since seeing her.

Jacob looked out over the Thames as his cab crossed Waterloo Bridge. The city on both banks was brilliantly lit in the night—the solid-looking Victorian offices and government buildings, the soaring skyscrapers, the giant Millennium Wheel all lit up, and a horde of rushing pedestrian and vehicular traffic. Jacob liked how London teemed with life. For a home, he preferred the rural idyll of his place outside of Athens, but visits to big cities always filled him with excitement. It was a shame that he wouldn't have a chance to enjoy any of London's nightlife.

Except for the sleaze pit he was going to visit right now.

He had the cab drop him off a couple of blocks from The Two Duelists and walked the rest of the way. In this business, you never take a cab straight to a sensitive location, and it's always good to get a feel for the neighborhood anyway.

The feel of the neighborhood was the same as the last time he'd been here.

He walked down a poorly lit street littered with trash. On either side stood old Victorian brick buildings and the occasional concrete replacement, put up after the Blitz or to satisfy the optimistic and ultimately fruitless dream of some developer who thought he could make something out of this area. The ground floors were taken up by second-rate businesses—grimy kebab shops, unlicensed taxi companies, Thai "massage" parlors, liquor stores, and discount stops for cheap Chinese imports. Upstairs were narrow windows with grimy, tattered curtains veiling grimy apartments and the tattered lives that lived in them.

But Jacob's eyes stayed mostly on the crowd, a mishmash of working-class English and immigrants from a dozen different countries. He caught conversations in English, Urdu, Somali, and Bengali. There were few women about, all of them accompanied by men. A crowd of a dozen burly Pakistanis stood on the street in tracksuits, the current style for street thugs in London, glowering at everyone who passed.

At least that gang wouldn't be in The Two Duelists. He'd once seen an Italian drinking at the bar get a bottle broken over his head for not being white enough.

And there it was up ahead, a shabby pub on a corner next to a burnt-out block of apartments and an all-night laundry with a puddle of puke blocking the front door. The Two Duelists had windows, but you couldn't see through them because they were covered with English flags. Not the UK Union Jack, but the red Cross of St. George on a white background. Some English people flew the flag out of patriotism. Some flew it to support the English national football team. Some flew it because they hated foreigners.

The owners of The Two Duelists were from the third category.

The sign above the door was one of those fake vintage pub signs you see all over the UK. It showed two bewigged men in hose and tricorner hats duking it out with swords. One has just been skewered by the other, blood spurting out of his chest and back.

Truth in advertising. While Jacob had never seen someone stabbed by a sword in this pub, he'd seen people stabbed by just about everything else.

Even a bicycle spoke through the eye. That had been a particularly nasty thing to witness.

Just as he got to the door, a pair of well-off men in their early twenties, looking as out of place as a pair of zebras, came out, looking nervous.

Jacob snorted. They didn't need to worry about The Two Duelists as long as they were buying and leaving. They had to worry about the neighborhood. Jacob gave them a fifty-fifty chance of getting mugged before they made the nearest Tube station.

Jacob pushed through the door and entered a large front room. It was almost empty, the splintered and scarred wooden floor only having a few puddles of beer and none of blood. Several tables were spaced around the room, and at each table sat a lone man with a beer in front of him, staring at their phone.

Drug dealers. You come in here, go up to the man who sells what you want, make the deal, and get gone, like those two clubber kids who just left. The guy with the jigsaw puzzle scars on his face sold ecstasy. The man in the center of the room giving him a cold stare sold opioid painkillers. The guy with the mohawk sold ketamine and Rohypnol. The fat guy in the corner sold speed. He obviously didn't use his own product.

Jacob walked straight across the room to the bar, where the impressively muscled barman wearing a dress shirt two sizes too small for him stared at him impassively.

"I'll take a beer and a shot of Jamison," Jacob said.

"We don't have Jamison."

"Then give me two beers."

The man nodded, poured a single beer, and reached under the counter. There was a soft click to Jacob's left, and a door labeled "Employees Only" opened. Using the right password got you temporary status as an employee.

Jacob handed over a fifty-pound note. The price to be a temporary employee. He grabbed his beer, hefting the weight of the pint glass in his hand. A handy weapon, especially if smashed into someone's face. "Glassing," they called it. Yes, the English had a verb for smashing a glass in someone's face. Jigsaw Man in the front room had obviously been glassed once upon a time. Jacob wondered what the other guy looked like.

He passed through the doorway and into an entirely different scene.

The back room was crowded with men talking in pairs or small groups. Most were burly thugs like those out front. Others were lean, smaller men who held themselves with feline poise. Those would be more dangerous. Then there were a few wealthier types, dressed down for the occasion but still recognizable as patrons and lenders due to their superior grooming and lack of visible scars. Each of these men had a tougher man by his side. You didn't come into a place like The Two Duelists without being able to protect yourself.

Despite the English flags adorning the pub exterior, Jacob heard a babble of different languages—English and various Scandinavian and Slavic tongues. He recognized a few Serbian arms dealers, one of whom was making a deal with a Norwegian oil baron. A few Russian guns-for-hire hung out nearby, hoping to be pulled into the deal. At one of the tables, a Ukrainian and Romanian mercenary were arm wrestling. Razors had been set upright in blocks of wood on the table to add a little fun to the match. A crowd was quaffing beer and cheering them on. Jacob took a sip of his own and continued to scan the room.

Then he saw him, the man who generally had some answers.

Timothy Harden, nicknamed "Hare Run," was a lean and wiry man with red hair and bright freckles. He got his nickname at the Olympics ten years ago when he snapped up gold medals in the hundred-meter dash and the 400-meter hurdles. An injury a couple of years later ended his athletic career, and heavy gambling debts put him in dire straits until he discovered being a runner for London's many illegal operations paid better than being a runner on the track. A go-between, messenger, and delivery man for sensitive packages, Harden had made quite a reputation and a fortune big enough to lose at the posh casinos in Monte Carlo.

He made that money because he never talked about the deals that he was involved in. That gave him a level of trust rare in the community and gave Jacob a big problem—how to learn what this guy knew.

Jacob moved over to speak with him.

CHAPTER SEVEN

As Jacob approached, Timmy Harden looked up from the arm-wrestling match, made eye contact, and moved away from the crowd to a clear area against one wall. He didn't sit at the nearby empty table. Harden never sat. He always looked ready to spring away in the blink of an eye.

"Hey, Timmy, remember me?" Jacob asked.

"Andy boy! How's my favorite Yank?"

Everyone here knew him as Andrew Winston.

"Good, how are you doing?"

Timmy's response got drowned out by a howl of pain followed by a burst of cheering and laughter. Jacob looked over his shoulder. The Romanian had just lost the arm-wrestling match and was clutching his hand as it gouged blood.

Timmy shrugged and chuckled. "You win some, you lose some."

"Yeah, well it's your night to win, Timmy. I need some information, and I think you can help."

Jacob slipped him two hundred pounds. That wasn't for information, that was just for asking for information. With Timmy "Hare Run" Harden, nothing came for free.

"Nice one. Ask away, Yank."

Jacob glanced around to make sure no one was eavesdropping. No one appeared to be, and with everyone babbling about the arm-wrestling competition and the loser letting out a string of Romanian swear words as he wrapped his hand in a bandage, Jacob didn't see how anyone could.

"There was a hit on an American university professor working at Durham University. The guy's name was Arnold Woburn. Might be an Israeli connection. I know you've worked in that area a lot. You know who might want to take him out?"

Everyone working in the business has a good poker face. If they don't, they don't last long, and Timmy had lasted for several years.

But poker faces aren't made of stone. It's nearly impossible to hide all your tells, and Jacob was an expert at detecting them.

Timmy didn't skip a beat. "Woburn? Haven't heard the name, but I did hear there was some sort of operation up in Durham." He took a big slug of his pint, curling his arm around to hide his eyes.

He didn't quite manage it, and Jacob saw his eyes dart around the room.

"You know who you need to talk to? Pavel, the Bulgarian merc over there drinking vodka shots with some newbie I don't know."

"Pavel is the guy with the shaved head and shoulders as wide as the Suez Canal?"

"That's the one."

"I'll go check him out, thanks." Jacob handed him another five hundred pounds.

Jacob walked slowly across the room. He had only been pretending not to know Pavel. He'd read his dossier. Specialized in protecting drug traffickers moving shipments from Eastern Europe. This guy was a bodyguard, not an assassin, and he didn't have any known connections to the Middle East.

Pavel didn't have anything to do with the case, and Timmy's shifty eyes proved it. He'd picked out someone in the room to distract Jacob.

Timmy would be sneaking off right about . . . *now*.

Jacob whirled around and saw Timmy heading out the door.

Jacob ran after him.

True to his name, by the time Jacob made it to the door leading to the front room, Timmy had already flashed across it and disappeared out the front door. Cursing, Jacob hurried to follow, then slipped on a puddle of beer left right inside the front door, probably by the little liar he was chasing. His feet slipped out from under him, his arms wheeled, and he nearly did a slapstick pratfall headfirst into a heroin dealer suspected of at least three murders.

Luckily for both himself, the dealer, and the general peace and security of The Two Duelists, that didn't happen. Jacob righted himself and got out the door.

Timmy was already a block down the street, sprinting so fast that he looked like he'd earn another gold medal.

There was no way Jacob was ever going to catch this guy on foot.

So, he wouldn't chase him on foot.

A food delivery driver was just passing by on his motorcycle, a big orange package on the back. Jacob cut him off, and the motorcyclist swerved to avoid him, screeching to a halt just before hitting a recycling bin.

"What the bloody hell do you think you're doing?" the delivery driver shouted.

Jacob grabbed him and flipped him off the bike, breaking his fall so that he didn't get hurt. He didn't like harassing innocent civilians like this, but lives were on the line.

He righted the motorcycle, hopped on, and got a punch in the face for being so nice about reducing collateral damage.

For a delivery driver, the guy had a hell of a right hook.

Jacob whipped out his gun from his concealed shoulder holster under his jacket.

That did the trick. The guy raised his hands and backed off.

"Sorry!" Jacob shouted, returning the gun to the holster and doing a quick 180 on the motorcycle.

He revved it up to eighty, weaving between traffic. Timmy came into view up ahead, still sprinting. Jacob felt something wet on his mouth. He touched it and came away with blood. He shrugged it off. His fault for robbing a delivery driver at gunpoint.

Timmy glanced over his shoulder and saw Jacob bearing down on him. He ducked down a side street, and Jacob followed.

It was a poorly lit residential lane with two-story houses on either side, most attached to one another to make a solid line of buildings. Jacob smiled. Timmy had run into a trap.

That smile faded when Timmy sprinted right up to one of the homes, leapt onto the little roof sheltering the front door, then leapt again to grab the gutter on the roof. With practiced ease, he swung himself up and onto the rooftop. Jacob got the impression that he'd scouted out this escape route beforehand just in case he wanted to dodge a question.

But why? Timmy had been a good source for all sorts of sensitive information. Why did he get so spooked about some wet work on the other side of the country?

Jacob ditched the bike on the small front lawn just as a curtain parted and a woman looked out. Great. More innocent bystanders. Jacob vaulted onto the rooftop over the door and leapt for the gutter.

That didn't work so well. Weakened by Timmy climbing up it, and now straining under the weight of a larger man, the gutter creaked and bent.

Jacob got just enough leverage off it to hoist himself up the final inches before it snapped.

He ended up holding onto the edge of the roof as the gutter collapsed, banging into his feet and almost tearing him off the roof. A shriek from the window told him the homeowner saw that.

"Sorry!" he shouted. He was having to apologize a lot tonight.

"I'm calling the police!"

"Of course you are."

He lifted himself up, swung a leg onto the roof, and clambered up onto the shingles.

By the time he got to the apex of the sloping roof, Timmy was several houses away, walking instead of running. He was a sprinter, not a tightrope walker, and he looked a bit uncertain of himself.

Good. Jacob started running along the connected rooftops. He wasn't a tightrope walker either, but he had less aversion to risk than Timmy.

No less vulnerability to it, though. A loose shingle sheared off under his foot, Jacob wheeled his arms, tottered at a heart-clenching angle, and finally righted himself.

Now Timmy was several houses ahead. Jacob decided to risk it all and run.

He didn't want to run on the apex of the roof, which had a smooth ridge that didn't give much purchase, so he ended up running on the steep incline to one side. If another shingle sheared off, he'd end up with a broken leg or worse.

Luckily that didn't happen. He began to close on Timmy.

The former Olympic runner noticed and realized that he needed to get on a better racetrack. Setting his feet wide, he edged down to the overhang above someone's back yard, grabbed onto the gutter, swung down, and dropped onto the grass.

Jacob cursed. He'd never catch him now.

Then a furious barking and a terrified yelp gave Jacob hope.

He ran to the spot where Timmy had descended and followed his path as the barking and yelping continuing.

Jacob got there just in time to see Timmy vault a fence, one sleeve shredded and a big tear out of the seat of his pants. A German Shepherd made a final snap at him before Timmy got safe.

Jacob ran parallel to him along the rooftop and then made a flying leap, tackling the smaller man and slamming him to the ground. The air went out of the runner in a loud gust. The barking continued from the next yard, and a window opened upstairs in the house of the back yard where they lay.

Not much time. Jacob got onto his knees, grabbed Timmy by the collar and shook him. "What do you know?"

Timmy's head lolled. The guy was pretending that he was dazed.

Maybe he really was dazed. A hard slap either woke him up or stopped his shamming.

"I . . . I don't know nothing," he gasped.

Another slap.

"I'm calling the police!" a man's voice shouted from the upper-story window.

"That's what your neighbor said!" Jacob called back over his shoulder, then he turned to Timmy. "All right. Spill."

"Imran Sanjrani."

"Who?" The name sounded Pakistani.

"He runs a mobile phone shop on Norwich Lane. It's a front. He arranges illegal passage into the country."

"Hold on." Jacob hauled him to his feet. The dog was still barking, and the guy upstairs was still watching them, phone in hand. Jacob led his prisoner along the side of the house to where a gate stood. Since they were on the inside, he could open it and lead Timmy to the street, carefully closing it behind him and making sure it locked. This was a bad neighborhood. You never knew what disreputable lowlifes might end up in your back yard.

They got to the street and kept on walking. No need to run. The police response time in this area was terrible.

"OK, tell me more."

"Imran Sanjrani is a fixer for a trafficking gang. Voluntary trafficking. No slave girls or anything like that, just illegal immigrants with the money to buy some help. It's a good operation. They always get their people through and never get caught. I heard they brought in a group of Americans and Europeans a couple of days ago. That's the kind of weird story that makes the rounds."

"I can imagine."

They had made it to a busier street. Jacob kept his arm around Timmy's shoulder to restrain him. To everyone else, they looked like old pals. Well, maybe more than pals considering the ripped seat of Timmy's pants.

"Then I heard from another source that these same blokes were behind the murder up in Durham."

"What else do you know?"

"That's all. I swear."

"OK, let's go to Sanjrani's mobile shop."

"I can't go there! If him and his crew know I grassed on them, they'll slit my throat!"

"Relax. I'll tie you up. I just have to make sure that you're telling the truth. If you are telling the truth, I'll let you go." Jacob's arm tightened into a headlock. "You *are* telling the truth, aren't you?"

"Y . . . yes," Timmy choked.

Jacob relaxed his grip but kept his arm around the runner's shoulders.

"Does he have a code word?"

"Better opportunities."

"Seems appropriate."

They got to Norwich Lane, which was a busy little side street lined with shops. Jacob grimaced. While this was the kind of neighborhood where people didn't see things, assuming you didn't run along their rooftops, he worried one of Imran Sanjrani's friends might be on watch.

He spotted the mobile phone shop up ahead, a narrow storefront with a brightly lit window showing off phones and phone cases. Nearby, but out of sight of the shop interior, stood a bicycle rack.

"Sit on the rack," Jacob ordered.

"Why?"

"Do it."

Timmy grumbled and did as he was told. Jacob pulled out a pair of handcuffs, shielding them from view of the passersby with his body. He handcuffed Timmy to the bike rack, and the runner edged down his sleeve to hide the steel around his wrist, then moved over to sit on the other end of the handcuffs, hiding them entirely.

"Atta boy," Jacob said with a grin, giving him a playful pat on the cheek. "I'll be right back and let you go, assuming you've told me the truth. Otherwise, I'll just leave you here."

Jacob strolled into the mobile phone shop.

Now for the hard part.

CHAPTER EIGHT

Jacob entered the shop, spotting a CCTV camera above the front door.

The interior was cramped, with walls lined with phone cases. Anything worth stealing, like ear buds and the phones themselves, were in a glass display counter or the locked window display. Wise move in this neighborhood. A corpulent Pakistani man sitting behind the counter talked to a customer about a burner phone. Jacob saw a lot of those for sale.

He pretended to look through the phone cases while actually studying the man behind the counter. He wore a loose, tan *shalwar kameez*, the traditional pants and long shirt worn in Pakistan, and had a matching skullcap.

A beard fringed his round face, but his upper lip was cleanly shaven. A popular style for the Salafists, a radical brand of Muslims who took things like Sharia law and jihad as literal instructions from Allah.

Was there an Islamist connection to all this? And if so, why were these Americans and Europeans involved?

Jacob caught Imran Sanjrani eyeing him. He pulled a phone case off the rack and compared it to the size of his phone. He put it back and pulled another phone case off the rack, waiting for his chance.

At last, the customer bought a burner and left. Jacob turned to Sanjrani.

"May I help you?" the Salafist asked.

Jacob returned the phone case to the rack. "A couple of people I know are looking for better opportunities."

Sanjrani's eyes sparked with interest. "There are good opportunities here in the UK."

"That's what they think. Can we talk?"

"One moment."

Sanjrani waddled out from behind the counter, locked the door and switched the sign to say, "back in ten minutes," then returned to his place behind the counter.

"Where are your friends coming from?"

Jacob opened his jacket a little to reveal his holster. "Put your hands on the counter, and don't make me show you how fast I can draw this. I watched way too many Westerns as a kid."

Sanjrani did as he was told, glowering at him. "I never keep much money here."

"Smart move. I'm not after money. I want to know about a group of Americans and Europeans you shipped in a few days ago. You might have heard they went up to Durham and killed a professor."

"I don't know what you're talking about."

"I can't even begin to count how many people I've killed."

"Death holds no fear for me."

Sanjrani's eyes said different.

"Selling burners and shipping illegal immigrants into the country isn't going to earn you seventy-two virgins. Unless these guys are fellow Salafists, you have no obligation to them."

"My professional reputation—"

"Is meaningless if you don't survive the night."

Sanjrani sighed, grumbled, and considered. Jacob gave him a moment.

"All right. I cannot give you names because we don't use real ones."

His eyes flicked downwards.

"Go on and keep those hands where I can see them."

Jacob moved around to the back of the counter. There was something covered in cloth on a shelf by Sanjrani's knees. Jacob removed it and saw a revolver. Tut-tutting, Jacob emptied the bullets into a trash can, pocketed the cylinder, and put the gun back in its place. He got back on his side of the counter.

"You were saying?"

"The one who came to me dressed like a businessman. He had an American accent but seemed familiar with London and the laws here. I think he lives here or has lived here. He needed to get several men into the country and then back out. All of them were American or European."

"That's not common for you, is it?"

"No, but if the money is good, I don't ask questions."

"Of course not. When did you get them out of the country?"

"Two days ago."

"Where did you send them?"

Pause.

"Imran, I'm not exactly law enforcement, but I know lots of people in law enforcement. How about I beat the crap out of you right now, handcuff you, and have the Metropolitan Police check out your human trafficking operation while detaining you for possession of an illegal firearm?"

"Son of a dog," Sanjrani muttered. "I hope you burn in eternal hellfire."

This was said in Urdu, so Jacob switched to Urdu. "If there's a hell, I'll probably be first in line, and I'll kick your ass when I see you down there. If you don't want an early trip downstairs, I suggest you tell me where you sent them."

"Israel," Sanjrani grunted.

Jacob snickered. "Israel? You do business with the Great Satan?"

"I live in one Great Satan, why not do business with another?"

"You people crack me up. Why did they want to go to Israel?"

"I don't know."

Jacob tapped his jacket where it covered his shoulder holster. "Do better."

"I don't know, but I did overhear something strange."

"What's that?"

"Two Frenchmen were among them, and they were speaking to each other in their own language. I know French. I lived there for a time."

"What did they say?"

"Something about finding the Ark."

"The what?"

"The Ark of the Covenant. That box the Jews kept their laws in."

"These guys wanted to find the Ark of the Covenant? That's the dumbest . . . oh wait."

Woburn had discovered some ancient papyri that talked about preserving holy artifacts. Then these guys killed him and headed to Israel.

To find the Ark of the Covenant?

These people were crazy. That thing hadn't been seen in two thousand years, assuming it ever existed in the first place.

But that was neither here nor there. If these people would kill someone to find the Ark, they'd kill again. And since there was no Ark to find, they'd just keep on killing.

He needed to get down to Israel.

"Did they mention where they were going once they got there?"

"Of course not."

"How many were there?"

"Besides the businessman who knew London? Eight."

"That must have been quite expensive, shipping these men in and out of the country."

Imran Sanjrani nodded.

Jacob thought about that. Nine people in total. Perhaps the whole team. Did they really all need to come here to beat up and kill one university professor? What else had they been doing here?

"What did these guys look like?" Jacob asked.

Sanjrani gave a general description of the nine men. Besides the businessman, all were young or early middle-aged, all white, and all fit. Sanjrani got the impression that they were all hardened underworld types. Jacob trusted his instinct on that one.

"You have a CCTV by the door, and probably another one hidden in here that I'm not spotting. Do you have footage of them?"

"It's automatically erased after twenty-four hours. Safer that way."

Jacob nodded. That made sense in case the police came looking. "Show me the computer."

Imran Sanjrani glowered at him, then turned the computer screen of his desktop to face him. Jacob grabbed the keyboard and, as the human trafficker cursed and sputtered, reformatted the hard drive.

"You don't want images of me on your computer," Jacob told him. "Safer that way."

Once the computer had finished reformatting, Jacob switched it off. "Now I'm going to walk out that door and you're going to pretend this conversation never happened. If you come after me, or anyone comes after me while I'm in London, me and some friends are coming back. You don't want that."

Sanjrani only nodded.

"See you," Jacob said brightly, heading out the door.

He went over to the bike rack where he had left Timmy, to find nothing but a set of handcuffs dangling from the rack.

"Huh," he muttered, staring at the empty cuffs. "Not many people know how to do that."

He reminded himself to put that in Timmy's dossier.

In the meantime, he had more important things to do.

CHAPTER NINE

Back at his hotel, Jacob talked to Tyler Wallace over in the Athens office via a secure server on his laptop. He told his boss everything that had happened so far, even the embarrassing details like his rooftop chase and Timmy finally giving him the slip. Wallace listened with open amusement.

"Sometimes I wish I was still working in the field," Wallace said with a chuckle once Jacob finished. "But only sometimes. The other times I remember all the crap I had to put up with. What you said about Israel is interesting. We just heard from an informant in the Israeli Defense Forces that a group of Negev Bedouin were found slaughtered in their camp. More than forty men, women, and children. A large sum of bloodstained cash was blowing around the site, and oddly, in a tent where most of the men had been shot, the soldiers found a collection of cheap French perfume."

"That's a weird detail."

"It gets weirder. On the floor of that same tent were a few beads of ANFO."

"Ammonium nitrate and fuel oil? Uh-oh. So, an explosives deal gone wrong?"

"That's what the IDF think."

"No casualties from the other side? I have a hard time believing a group of Bedouin would be taken that much by surprise."

"They probably weren't. The Bedouin had been dead for at least twenty-four hours, and the weather has been windy. Any tracks would have disappeared. The other side might have buried their dead in the sand and all trace of it is now gone."

"So, you're thinking that our little group of historian killers might have done this too?"

"My gut says yes."

If Wallace's gut said something, Jacob listened. Wallace started doing this stuff when Jacob was still borrowing his dad's car so he could get his girlfriend to join him in the back seat.

"And why does your gut think that?"

"Because it doesn't fit. Just like the murder of a historian doesn't fit. And your phone salesman friend sent them to Israel. I'd bet my pension those two crimes are connected."

Jacob smiled. "Your pension? That's not a very big bet. Can you get me a quick flight to Israel?"

"Sure, but that's about all I'm going to be able to get you when you come to me with a story like that, and all I can back it up with is a hunch."

"Alone again, huh? Story of my life."

For some reason, that made him have a thought. "I think I need to go back to Morocco first."

"Morocco? Why?"

"There's an expert there who might be able to help me with some intel."

Wallace studied him for a moment. "Dr. Peters."

"Um, yeah." It sure was hot in this hotel room. Stuffy. It was making his face get red.

"And you think she might have a lead on this?"

"She's the only person familiar with the historical period who I can trust to ask. Plus, she reads Hebrew. She might get more out of those archaeological reports than I did."

"Very well. Since we don't have any leads yet on the Bedouin attack, that might be the best course of action. Also check into whether there's a Sword of the Righteous connection."

"We stomped them pretty good on the last mission."

"Yes, but as you know, they're down but not out. Our Egyptian allies eliminated the cells there, but there are outposts in Algeria and Libya, and they're recruiting again."

Jacob grunted. He and Jana had intercepted a cell of that terror group trying to set off a crude nuclear device in the Suez Canal. They stopped them, but only at the expense of disabling the cargo ship the group had been transporting it on and blocking the canal for a week, at the cost of hundreds of millions in lost revenue. The attack made international headlines, the US and Egyptian secret services keeping the nuclear device out of the story. That would have made an even bigger impact.

The impact was bad enough as it was. A disruption on that big of a scale, along with the killing of several members of the Egyptian armed forces, had made the group into terrorist superstars. Even losing so many men, they would probably emerge stronger from this.

"Do you think they could have recruited a team of Americans and Europeans?" Jacob asked.

"I don't see why not," Wallace said. He was looking down and typing. "There are reports of a Frenchman and a Canadian in the cell in Algeria. I'll send over the info. I'm also getting your plane. Hold on."

A moment more of typing. Jacob relaxed a little. Wallace was the dream boss. Efficient and open to crazy ideas, like a terrorist group going after the Ark of the Covenant. Well, after a terrorist group went after an ancient Egyptian canopic jar holding natural plutonium, why shouldn't he?

If only everyone in the CIA could be so open-minded. Wallace had been a field agent for decades and knew that the situation out in the world didn't always fit the neat little boxes the think tanks and analysts in Washington dreamed up.

Wallace finished typing and looked at the screen.

"You need to get to Heathrow Airport pronto. I got you on a military transport leaving in an hour that's going to Gibraltar. From there, I'll arrange a smaller plane to take you to Asilah."

"Thanks."

"Good luck. I'll keep monitoring the situation with the Bedouin attack and feed you intel as soon as I get it. I'm afraid the Israeli government isn't going to be too helpful with this. Fights between Bedouin groups are only too common, and even a massacre like this isn't unknown."

"That's more among the city Palestinians than the nomad Bedouins."

Every year or so, there'd be a honor, revenge killing where one family would attack another, usually at a wedding or funeral where a bunch of people would gather and make an easier target.

"Sure, but the government doesn't perceive much of a difference between the two groups," Wallace said.

"Which is why they still have so many problems with both of them."

"Maybe so. In any case, they're investigating this as a tribal rivalry, although the traces of ANFO have them spooked."

"Good. A spooked Israeli is a vigilant Israeli. Hopefully, they're get their investigation on the right track sooner rather than later."

"I'll work on them," Wallace said. "Talk to you soon, Jacob."

* * *

Two hours later, sitting in an uncomfortable seat in the back of a US Airforce transport plane flying over Spain on its way to Gibraltar, Jacob looked through the dossier Wallace had sent him.

He felt uneasy heading to Morocco when the action seemed to be taking place in Israel, clear on the other side of the Mediterranean, but he needed to talk to Jana. There was nothing to see at the attack site in the Negev. It would be swarming with Israeli police and military, and even though the CIA had a good working relationship with them, there was nothing Jacob could find there that the investigators couldn't. He'd have to wait for their report. Wallace would get it for him. He always came through with stuff like that.

As he read through the dossier, he began to think going to the Magreb instead of the Levant might not be taking him off track after all.

While The Sword of the Righteous hadn't been as active or successful at recruiting Westerners as ISIS, they'd been ramping up their efforts. The Algerian cell had been especially good at that, recruiting several French and Francophone Canadians. Most were of Algerian heritage, but two were of an entirely different character.

One was a small-time French criminal who switched from stealing cars to waging jihad after being converted. That was not unusual. Angry young men with a history of trouble with the law often ended up radicalized. A white Frenchman was more likely to join some Neo-Nazi group, since he was more likely to come across that ideology in his neighborhood than radical Islam, but in recent years, an increasing number of native Europeans were drifting in that direction thanks to slick online recruiting drives.

The French-Canadian was of more serious concern. He had earned a master's degree in civil engineering and worked for the Quebec Highway Department for five years before converting, quitting his job, and leaving the country. His movements were unclear for a few years, but the State Department had found evidence that he had gone to a terrorist training center in Pakistan run by Al Qaeda before deciding to leave that weakened operation and shifting to the more active Sword of the Righteous.

Intel now firmly located him in Algeria, as good a place as Pakistan for a terrorist to base himself. While the native languages were Arabic and Berber, most people spoke at least some French in the former French colony, making it an easy choice for the two Westerners.

Algeria had a fairly democratic government at the moment, but it struggled with corruption and an inability to extend much power into the Sahara, the southern four-fifths of the nation that was a Wild West of Islamist groups, tribal militias, and rebels of all stripes.

Besides hunkering down in bases in a few major towns and controlling the roads during daylight hours, the Algerian army couldn't do much. There were simply too many lawless elements in too big a space.

The Sword of the Righteous had a desert training camp in the Béchar Province, a sparsely inhabited stretch of scrub and grasses on the northern fringe of the Sahara. While it was a bit too north for comfort in that it was only about a hundred kilometers away from the government's zone of total control, it benefitted from being cut by rough mountains and wide stretches of roadless waste. Only Bedouin and a few poor villagers survived here. The sparse vegetation and minimal rainfall meant there were no farmers, only herders, and the lack of mineral deposits meant the Algerian army focused its show of force on more important areas.

The only exception to this was in the extreme west of the province, which had a border with Morocco. The Algerian army had a whole string of outposts there.

Jacob couldn't help but think that had been part of the terrorists' planning. Morocco had a king who took a dim view of Islamists. He didn't make deals with them like some African and Middle Eastern leaders. An unsung hero like General Jaloul Cherkaoui in Marrakesh could never exist in Algeria. Maybe The Sword of the Righteous were planning to strike across the border?

So, after getting some guidance from Jana, his next move was probably to sneak across the Moroccan-Algerian border and strike that Sword of the Righteous base. It was overdue for an ass kicking. He figured the two Westerners were gone, but if he could grab a couple of prisoners, he could find out what their target was.

Jacob put away the dossier and closed his eyes. There was another hour before he got to Gibraltar. Best to catch some sleep while he could.

Through long training, he could drop off at a moment's notice. What wasn't part of his training were the dreams he had of Jana.

When he awoke with the wheels touching down at the RAF base in Gibraltar, the dream dissipated from his mind. All he was left with was a warm feeling in his chest, a tight feeling in his pants, and one vivid image of her diving naked from his boat into the clear blue Aegean Sea.

CHAPTER TEN

Jana snapped awake instantly, sitting bolt upright in bed, her hand on a hammer she kept on a wooden crate that served as her bedside table.

The tent was pitch black. The moon had set, and the sun hadn't yet sent its first rays to lighten the east. The camp was quiet.

But something had awakened her.

She had no idea what. Some sound, something different than the occasional cry of a night bird or steady pace of the policemen doing their rounds as they watched the camp and archaeological site through the night.

Slowly, she curled her fingers around the hammer and lifted it off the bedside table. Ever since that attack on the hillside, she had been jittery. The Moroccan police had investigated and couldn't figure out why some unknown man had been killed near their excavation site with gunshots and a grenade. Jana could have filled them in but wasn't allowed to.

At least the local police chief had assigned them a second night watchman. Both now carried Kalashnikovs instead of the standard revolvers.

Could it be this new guy prowling around her tent? Some lonely cop with exaggerated views of the availability and willingness of Western women?

A smack on the head with a hammer would dampen his lust. She stared into the darkness, willing her eyes to see.

A sound came to her, so faint that it barely intruded on the edge of her hearing.

The soft scrape of cloth on cloth.

Clothing on the lower edge of her canvas tent? Was someone crawling under her tent? Had it been the sound of a tent peg being pulled up that had roused her?

Time to get the show on the road.

She groped around for her flashlight, which she also kept on her bedside table, grabbing it just as she heard the noise a second time.

Heart beating fast, not daring to kick off the covers for fear that the intruder would hear, she pointed the flashlight in the direction of the sound and raised her hammer to strike.

She clicked on the flashlight, leaping from her bed at the same time.

A male form crouched at the foot of her bed. She brought the hammer down . . .

. . . and then stopped.

It was Jacob Snow.

"Jesus!" she whispered. "You scared the crap out of me. What are you doing here?"

Jacob put a finger to his lips. "Shhh. One of the cops isn't far off."

"You snuck past him?"

"Easy."

"What about the secret agents they supposedly sent to guard the perimeter?" Jana hadn't seen any evidence that they were there.

"I had some tea with them on the way in."

Jacob got up with a grin and sat on the edge of her bed. Jana stared. Even stranger than his sudden reappearance was the fact that he had an archaeological field report tucked under his arm.

"What's going on? Is there going to be another hit on me?"

"No, we don't have any intel to say another assassin is on his way, and don't worry, the two agents out there are top tier. I've got something a bit more archaeological to talk to you about." He raised the excavation report. "Why don't you put on some pants, and I'll tell you."

Jana realized that she was standing there only in a halter top and panties. For a moment, she had an urge to keep standing there just as she was, then she blushed and grabbed a pair of shorts.

Jacob's eyes never left her. With most guys that would have earned them a slap, especially after sneaking into her tent, but Jacob must have his reasons.

For the sneaking into the tent part.

"So, what's going on?" she asked once she was dressed. She sat on the other end of the bed.

"I went up to Durham University to investigate that colleague of yours. There was some chatter that he was taken out by a terror group."

Jana hung her head. *Taken out.* It made his murder sound so impersonal, almost cool. But Arnold Woburn hadn't been some NPC in a video game. He had been a colleague. While not a friend, she had enjoyed several interesting conversations with him at conferences over the years.

"Sorry," Jacob added. "That was badly said."

"It's all right."

She couldn't really expect anything more from a CIA agent. This was the same organization that kept her father from her as she was growing up, and then eventually got him killed.

Jacob set the archaeological report on the bed between them. "I got this from Woburn's office. It's about an excavation at Tel Shimon he was on a few years back. His boss says the Israeli government wouldn't let him publish a papyrus he found. There's a mention in here that the papyri included instructions for the care of Jewish holy artifacts and how to keep them hidden from the Romans during the Bar Kokhba rebellion. But when I skimmed through the texts, I didn't see any papyrus about that. I'm thinking that's what got censored."

"The Israelis are sensitive about that sort of thing," Jana said, picking up the heavy volumes.

"That's what Woburn's boss said. And I traced the men who killed him, at least partway. They entered the UK illegally, which means they're either on a terrorism watch list or they didn't want to appear in the records at all. They used the same trafficker to leave and headed to Israel."

"Israel?"

"Yeah, and the trafficker overheard them talking. Said they were after nothing less than the Ark of the Covenant."

"That's ridiculous. It might never have even existed, and if it did, it's been lost for millennia."

Despite her professional skepticism, she felt a strange thrill go through her—that old familiar excitement of discovery. She had felt it when her crew had uncovered the mosaic and felt it again when she and Jacob learned of a canopic jar that held natural plutonium.

That thrill was what got her into archaeology. It was what she lived for.

She started flipping through the archaeological report. Woburn and his team had dug through several layers of occupation on Tel Shimon to get to the burn layer of the Bar Kokhba period, finding evidence of a siege, including several large arrowheads fired by ballistae, giant crossbows used by the Romans. A ramp, much eroded over the centuries, led up to the city wall atop the tel so the Romans could bring up their siege engines. The wall at that point had been battered down, and every building inside was burned and collapsed. They had even found several skeletons buried in the rubble.

The tel had remained uninhabited for several hundred years after that, the rubble settling, windblown dirt filling the cracks and weeds no doubt growing atop the scene of the massacre. When people started resettling Tel Shimon in the Byzantine and later Muslim periods, they had simply built atop these ruins, not knowing they were living on top of a mass grave.

Jana shuddered. As a scientist, she was supposed to retain a professional detachment to the past, but evidence of such ancient drama always moved her.

And she was getting swept up in that drama. She found the artifact that Jacob had referred to: a sealed amphora, a type of vessel used by the Greeks and Romans to store wine. But instead of wine, it had been filled with documents written on papyrus.

A lucky find, although not a unique one. Twice, caches of documents from the period had been found in caves. In one cave, called the Cave of Letters, investigators found letters written by the rebel leader himself, as well as a fascinating collection of business correspondence from a female landowner named Babatha. The nearby Cave of Horror, so named because forty men, women, and children were buried inside, contained more letters and fragments of holy script.

The find at Tel Shimon was equally important. She had read the initial report at the time but had no idea that the Israeli government had confiscated one of the texts. She didn't know Woburn all that well, and he had never confided in her.

"Finding anything?" Jacob asked.

"I'm still reading."

"If you're going to be reading for long, do you mind if I take a nap? It's been a long trip."

A voice from outside in Arabic interrupted them. "Is everything all right, miss?"

The watchman. Jana blushed. He must have heard a male voice inside her tent.

"Yes, Sergeant Bensaid. Everything's fine."

She heard him walk away. "He's going to be gossiping to all the other policemen tomorrow," Jana grumbled.

"Sorry." Jacob stretched out on her camp bed and was instantly asleep. Jana rolled her eyes. Her father could do that too. A lot of soldiers could.

As Jacob snored loudly, announcing to the entire camp that a guy was in her tent, she read through the archaeological report. She found the passage Jacob had pointed out, a mention that the amphora contained a papyrus that detailed the preservation of holy artifacts, but no mention of that in the text.

She skimmed through the rest of the report. Jacob had underestimated his ability to understand Hebrew. He'd gotten all the information there was to be gotten from the report.

Jana turned to look at him. Lying sprawled on her bed, mouth hanging open, and emitting a sound that would scare a pack of hyenas, he wasn't the most attractive sight, but having him sleeping beside her while she read gave her a warm, almost domestic feeling.

She shook her head. Domesticity? That wasn't how she rolled, and it sure wasn't how Jacob Snow rolled.

She shook him awake. His eyes snapped open, and he was alert in an instant. Jana recoiled. Her dad used to do that, too, and it always freaked her out.

"What's wrong?" he asked, sitting up.

"Nothing, except you were snoring to wake the dead. When you're on an operation, doesn't that give you away to the enemy?"

"I sleep on my side," he said as he rubbed his eyes.

"What if you roll onto your back?"

"I don't."

"Well, next time you fall asleep in my tent, pretend you're in enemy territory, and take your boots off too, you got dirt on my blankets."

"Can't. Got to be ready at all times."

"Whatever," she said, brushing the dirt off her bed. "I read through the report and didn't find anything new."

"Damn. You wouldn't happen to know where the Ark of the Covenant is, would you?"

"Yeah, right. There are a lot of theories. The main one is that it's in Axum, in Ethiopia. The Ethiopian Orthodox Church is one of the oldest organized churches in existence, and they have a tradition that at their cathedral in northern Ethiopia, they guard the Ark."

"There's no evidence the group is going to Ethiopia."

"And there's no real evidence that the Ethiopians have the Ark. In fact, all Ethiopian churches have a replica Ark in the holy of the holies behind the altar. Most likely the one in Axum is just an older example of this."

"Could it be in Israel?"

"Some traditions state that it was hidden in the desert somewhere to keep it safe from the Romans. Others claim that it was buried in a secret chamber in the Temple Mount."

"Really?"

Jana shook her head. "It's not there. The Temple Mount has been thoroughly documented and studied ever since the foundation of the state of Israel. And before that, it was probed by European archaeologists, treasure hunters, and just about everyone else. If there were any secret chambers, they would have been discovered long ago."

"But what about beneath the Temple Mount? I mean, the Mount is basically the ruins of Solomon's Temple, right? What if it's below that, not in a chamber of the temple itself, but in the temple's basement?"

"There were two Temples, both on the same site one after another. All that area has been probed. Lots of people have had that idea."

Jacob thought for a moment. "Could the Israeli government already have it? They keep sensitive documents for themselves, so why not the Ark? Maybe they discovered it, didn't tell anyone, and locked it away. The group acquired some ammonium nitrate and fuel oil, an explosive. What if they plan to blast into the Israeli equivalent of Fort Knox?"

"I suppose that's possible. More likely, they don't have the Ark at all, and this group is just following a conspiracy theory."

"A conspiracy theory that will get a lot of people killed." Jacob stood. "Thanks. I need to get going."

Jana blinked. "Wait. I'm not coming with you?"

"Of course not. The Egypt mission was a one-off. You know that."

"But you might need my help."

"You've already helped a lot."

"Where are you going?"

"Some of the group were Francophone. We've gotten intel that a couple of Francophone Westerners joined our old friends The Sword of the Righteous. Apparently, they are in a desert training camp in Algeria's Béchar Province or were. I'm going to check it out."

"Alone?"

Jacob gave her a hard look. "Yes, alone. Now, I really need to go. It been good to—I mean, thanks for the help."

He unzipped the tent a little, peeked out, then disappeared into the night.

Leaving Jana alone, facing a decision.

CHAPTER ELEVEN

The sun dawned over a bleak, rocky plain. Jacob rattled along in a Jeep, feeling like the fillings in his teeth would shake out at any moment.

He was driving along the *hamada*, a stony highland common in the Algerian desert where all the sand had blown away or trickled between the stones, leaving nothing behind but a bone-jarring rough surface to drive over. The stones were volcanic, and their black surfaces absorbed the heat. He would see no Bedouin here, the stones too hot for their camels' feet. His Jeep was fitted with special tires that wouldn't dry out and crack from the searing surface. He could feel the heat like a wave rising off the desert floor.

Jacob wore a *keffiyeh*, the traditional headscarf favored by the Bedouin, and with his deeply tanned skin, someone would mistake him for a local from a distance.

But there was no one to see him here. The Moroccan government had led him to an isolated spot on the border that they knew had recently been passed by an Algerian patrol that wouldn't come that way again for another day, and he had slipped effortlessly across to Algeria.

Relations between the two nations were so bad that the Moroccans were more than happy to help.

Jacob watched the surrounding terrain with a sharp eye. Speeding along an almost featureless plain, with only distant mountains to the north and south, it wasn't like he had to keep his eye on the road.

No, he had to keep his eye on everything else. The Algerian army patrols may not be close, but this was Sword of the Righteous territory, and Wallace had told him the latest intel indicated that Al Qaeda of the Islamic Magreb was trying to push into this area. Al Qaeda had been smacked down pretty hard by the Algerian government and had expanded into softer targets like Mali and Niger. Now, they wanted to come back.

Good. After he hit the Sword of the Righteous base, maybe their central command would think Al Qaeda did it and strike back. Nothing better than two Islamist armies fighting each other, giving the civilized world some breathing space.

He saw no one—no patrols, no militias, and no Bedouin—and yet an uneasy feeling plagued him all that morning, and he kept looking over his shoulder directly behind him.

There was nothing there. At one point, he even stopped the Jeep, stood on its hood, and studied the horizon with a powerful pair of binoculars. Still nothing.

I'm getting jittery. Maybe Wallace is right, maybe I should have taken a longer vacation.

He thought that it had been long enough. Three weeks sailing in the Aegean, part of it accompanied by his casual girlfriend Gabriella Cremonesi, a gorgeous Italian documentary and wildlife photographer a good ten years younger than him. That was a bit too much of an age gap, but it meant that she wasn't serious about anything long-term, which was just as well with a guy like him.

It sure was nice watching her dive off the ship into those blue waters, though.

Wait. Didn't he have a dream about that recently?

Oh yeah, and his subconscious had replaced Gabriella with Jana.

Get your ass back behind the steering wheel.

Shaking his head, he headed east across the desert. No time for inappropriate daydreams. He had an appointment with The Sword of the Righteous.

* * *

The terrorist base was well-hidden from the air, and barely visible from the ground until you got in close. It stood half a mile down a narrow ravine, fifty-foot cliffs rising to either side. One portion of the ravine had some strange geology, with a band of softer rock running along the bottom. In ancient times, there had been a river here, which had scoured out this cut into the low mountains but had especially taken away this lower deposit. That left a deep overhang on either side of the canyon.

It was here that The Sword of the Righteous had built their base, stringing out tents and a couple of prefab structures in the shelter of the overhangs. Jacob hadn't seen this; he only knew this because the dumbasses had revealed their position by filming a beheading video there. They had captured Francois Garrier, an aid worker whose only crime had been to teach Algerian villagers who lacked electricity how to construct and use solar ovens. A Frenchman trying to teach

Algerians anything that improved their lives was an act punishable by death according to the terrorists, so they had abducted him from a rural village, killing three locals as they did so, and dragged him here, where they could kill him at their leisure.

What these guys didn't know was that the geology of their hideout was so unique that a geologist working with the CIA had been able to pinpoint it. The CIA had been about to pass along the intel to the Algerians, but they figured Jacob Snow would be better than any Algerian army platoon.

He intended to prove them right.

But first he had to get in.

He waited until nightfall.

The ravine was too rough to drive into, and near the opening, hidden beneath a series of tarps the same color as the desert held up by rods, were the group's vehicles.

Jacob studied them from half a mile off through night vision goggles.

He counted two Hummers, a truck, and three Technicals, Jeeps mounted with machine guns or light cannon, a cheap and effective form of mobile artillery for desert fighting. A pair of guards squatted nearby, the steam from their teacups making bright points in their hands. A faint glow from behind one of the trucks showed the location of a campfire. There was probably at least one more guard next to it.

The fire was a small one. Without his night vision goggles, he could barely see the glow at this distance, hidden as it was by the truck.

Still, it showed a lack of vigilance. Being close to the fire, the sentries' night vision would be hampered. These guys were not expecting trouble. Out in the middle of nowhere with a perfect hiding place, posting a watch was only a matter of routine for them.

Jacob was going to show them that they were wrong.

He began to creep forward.

Strapped across his back was a Kalashnikov. There were better assault rifles on the market, but he had picked the AK-47 because he wanted the wounds to be consistent with a rival militia or terrorist group. In his pouches across his vest were several grenades, and a 9-mm pistol was in his hip holster. In a sheath, he had a Bowie knife.

Jacob was stuck with a bad tactical situation. If he took out the sentries, then everyone in that fortress of a canyon would be alerted, and he'd have an impossible fight on his hands. If he slipped past the sentries and took out the main base, he'd be bottled up in the canyon with at least three sentries blocking his escape route.

Of course, he could try and kill the sentries silently, but with three men within calling distance of one another and perhaps more lurking between the vehicles, that was even riskier than the other options.

He decided to sneak into the main base and deal with the sentries later.

The vehicles were parked on flat ground a little away and to one side of the canyon mouth. The terrain directly in front of the entrance to the canyon was rough, a jumble of stones brought down by water action thousands of years ago when the Sahara was savannah instead of wasteland.

That gave him room to maneuver, but also meant loose rocks could shift and give away his position.

He edged along as far from the vehicles as possible. Moving slowly, Jacob tested each stone before trusting it with his weight. The sentries remained silent. His night vision flared up as one of them lit a cigarette.

It was a slow, painstaking process, but at last, he got into the canyon and out of sight of the vehicles and their watchmen.

Here he paused. The canyon looked ghostly in the green glow of his night vision goggles. The canyon walls bowed out to either side, each face having a half-circle weathered out of it about ten feet deep and twelve high before the rock changed and the walls rose almost sheer. The canyon wasn't terribly wide, and if anyone came along with a light, they'd spot him for sure.

But he could see no one. The canyon stretched out ahead, gradually turning so anything beyond a couple of hundred yards remained out of sight.

He began to rethink his strategy. If the sentries were this isolated, perhaps he should take them out?

No. All it would take would be for one sentry to fire one shot, and the sound would echo down to the main camp. No doubt, they had walkie-talkies too.

He'd have to go ahead and take out the main camp like he'd planned.

Continuing forward, AK-47 leveled, eyes and ears sharp, Jacob began to come around the turn. From what he remembered from the satellite photos, he'd be coming into view of the camp soon.

A light shone up ahead, growing brighter. Jacob stopped. The faint sounds of approaching footsteps told him that he might not achieve the surprise he thought he would.

Working fast, he pulled out a thin tarp from his vest pocket, covered himself with it, and lay on the ground.

The tarp was painted the same color as the local stone, complete with darker splotches to imitate shadows. Lying prone, with one shoulder and the opposite elbow poking up slightly to give the fake stone some shape, Jacob became motionless. From a distance or in poor light, it would trick the causal observer, but Jacob worried that having walked this route countless times, the terrorist or terrorists coming his way might notice a heap of stones that hadn't been there before.

Jacob peered out of a thin gap between the tarp and the ground, tense and waiting.

A lone figure strolled into view, carrying a flashlight, AK-47 slung casually on his back. He walked down the center of the ravine, where the ground was the clearest, but even so, he shone the light at his feet to keep from tripping on the loose stones.

The man passed. Jacob waited until his footsteps faded in the distance before he rose. Abandoning the tarp, he moved forward again.

Now, he could hear low voices ahead, the crackle of a campfire, and the hiss of a radio.

Jacob crouched. Now came the hard part. There was no way he was going to slip into a lit and busy camp. He'd penetrate as much as possible, and then it would be game time.

The problem was, he didn't know how many guys were in there.

He wished he had brought a rocket launcher. He wished he had brought some Moroccan commandoes.

But he hadn't been offered a rocket launcher, and there was no way a team of Moroccan commandoes would conduct an operation on Algerian soil.

So, he was alone, no better armed than his adversaries, and surrounded.

But he had the element of surprise, and he intended on using it.

He advanced at a slow squat. As the light grew, he pulled off his night vision goggles and set them on the ground.

The first campfire came into view. As he rounded the bend, he could see a fire set beneath the overhang to his left. Half a dozen men stood or squatted around it. Beyond them were a line of tents, a field kitchen, and several crates stacked up.

He knew the canyon straightened out right after this point, but he wouldn't get to see what was beyond it until he got past these guys. He wouldn't know the tactical situation until it smacked him in the face.

The time for stealth was over. While the men were in the firelight and he was in the relative darkness, it was only a matter of time before they saw him creeping up on them.

Time to get this show on the road. Jacob pulled a pin out of one of the fragmentation grenades and started sprinting for the campfire.

When they all turned at the noise, he threw the grenade right in the center of the crowd.

CHAPTER TWELVE

The grenade detonated right in the campfire, sending shrapnel, bits of wood, stones, and flames in all directions.

All six of the men around the fire went down, thrown back in red ruin to thump against the canyon floor and not rise.

Jacob didn't even look at them twice. He was already tossing a grenade at the cluster of tents just beyond. The canvas was shredded from his first grenade, but with the people inside probably lying prone, he couldn't bank on them all being killed or injured.

The second blast leveled every tent within sight. Jacob hit the dirt, worried the crates beyond might hold ammo and go off.

He rolled to the right to get some more distance between himself and danger, then pulled out a third grenade. When the crates didn't blow, he sprang back up and sprinted forward, rounding the bend, and coming to the straight part of the camp.

What he saw did not fill him with confidence.

Tents and a couple of prefab huts lined both sides of the canyon. Three more fires burned, two to the left and one near the end of the canyon to the right. Men swarmed out of tents or rose from their places around the fires, picking up arms and preparing for battle.

Jacob tossed his grenade at the nearest cluster of men, then went prone as the first fire began to come his direction. He unslung his AK-47, rolled to avoid some fire smacking off the stones nearby, then rolled again as one of the terrorists zeroed in on him.

He took out the guy with the best aim, then his buddy right next to him.

The fire increased. The terrorists were still confused, some only half awake, and the screams of the wounded and the scattered flames from the exploded campfires overloaded their senses, but the fighters from The Sword of the Righteous were all veterans, and they began to focus their fire on the lone man who seemed to be responsible for all this mayhem.

As a bullet plucked his collar, coming within a fraction of an inch of his flesh, Jacob realized that he could not keep this up for long.

Didn't Jana call me arrogant once? Maybe I am. Maybe that's going to get me killed.

Not today.

He noticed a pair of mortars standing just beyond the line of tents to the left. Next to them was a stack of metal ammo crates. If he could hit those, this whole canyon would become one hell of a fireworks show.

Speaking of fireworks shows, one guy in the approaching crowd got down on one knee, a rocket-propelled grenade launcher resting on his shoulder.

Jacob took him out, and the guy right behind him dove for the weapon as the first guy dropped it and then had to dive behind a large rock on the far-right side of the canyon as more fire chased him.

The rock was big enough to keep him safe for the moment, but the move brought him even further away from the stack of ammo. No way he could hit it with an AK-47 at this range, not when he couldn't peek over his rock for more than half a second without getting his head blown off.

He switched to full auto and sprayed the area. That got the terrorists to hunker down long enough for him to snap in another magazine and take a quick stock of the situation.

A ragged line of about twenty men had advanced, a few stragglers taking up the rear. Within a few more seconds, they'd start flanking his rock, and he wouldn't have any cover anymore.

He had to hit those ammo crates now, or he was sunk.

Grab the RPG? That would mean charging into the mass of men who were much closer to the weapon than he was.

Time for a distraction. As bullets cracked off the rock in increasing frequency, Jacob pulled out two smoke grenades and a fragmentation grenade. He lined them up, then flinched as a bullet hit the ground right next to his hand.

Behind the rock. How the hell did that happen?

Oh. The radicals were getting smart and hitting the overhang above his position, trying to angle ricochets down on him.

Another shot striking the ground near his leg told him he better hurry up with his plan.

Jacob pulled the pins and tossed the grenades in rapid succession. First the frag grenade right in the area where the RPG lay. He just had to hope no shrapnel hit the weapon or his plan was over before it got started. The two smoke grenades went left and right a moment later.

The blast in the center took out another couple of terrorists, and the smoke that burst to his flanks gave him cover as he grabbed his AK-47, leapt over the rock, and sprinted for the RPG.

The smoke cover wasn't complete, and these guys had a good idea where he was anyway, so as he charged, nearly doubled over to make as small a target as possible, bullets whined through the air all around him.

Also, the smoke screen directly in front of him was just a thin veil wafting in from the edges of both flanks, and a couple of stragglers way back in the canyon could see him perfectly well.

One did the old "spray and pray" with his Kalashnikov on full auto. He didn't hit anywhere close, and Jacob gave even odds that he might have hit a fellow jihadist hidden in the smoke.

The second guy was smarter. He had a rifle with a scope, and he'd gotten down on one knee and was aiming with calm care right at him.

Jacob sent a three-round burst at him and tucked into a roll. The guy didn't get hit and didn't flinch, but his bullet punched air just where Jacob had been a moment before.

Jacob kept rolling toward the RPG. The rifleman fired again, and Jacob's AK-47 was snatched from his hands as the bullet impacted the stock.

His roll banged to a stop against a jagged stone. Jacob leapt up to the right, then swerved to the left just before the rifleman's third bullet opened up his head, then dove for the RPG.

Which was unloaded. Great.

He grabbed it, then rolled over the corpse of its owner to get some cover. A bullet thumped into the dead flesh. Jacob reached around and got one of the slim projectiles that went into the launcher.

Jacob snapped it into place and peeked over the dead body. Both the rifleman and his more impulsive comrade in jihad were reloading. The smoke was still thick to either side of him, and the fire had died down, the terrorists unsure where to aim. A couple more were just running into view out of the back of the cloud to his left.

The pile of ammo next to the mortars was in plain sight. Jacob leveled the RPG, risked his life to aim for a second, and fired.

Then he hit the deck in the hopes of surviving the hell to come.

Jacob was not disappointed. The RPG slammed into the ammo crates and detonated.

Like he hoped, that set off a chain reaction.

An ear-splitting roar shook the ravine, followed by secondary explosions as mortar shells flew in all directions, smashing into the cliffs to either side and going off. A rumble of falling stone added to the din.

Jacob scrambled to the far right of the canyon, getting under the overhang in the desperate hope that it might shelter him. There was nowhere else to hide. He curled up in a tight ball, getting bounced by the reverberations of the relentless explosions. Sharp stones struck him, and he felt the hot kiss of shrapnel slice his calf. He curled into himself even more tightly, his mind a blank, erased by the overpowering noise and constant vibration.

At last, the shaking stopped, and the only sound was a deafening ringing in Jacob's ears. He lay curled up for a minute longer, not daring to think that the storm had passed, and he had survived it, and then he peeked between gritty fingers . . .

. . . and saw nothing.

A dun haze hung over the camp, garishly backlit by numerous fires.

Jacob crouched down, then winced and almost fell as the pain from the shrapnel wound in his calf broke through his shock. He glanced at it, saw that it was shallow enough to ignore for the moment, and grabbed the nearest Kalashnikov.

He tossed it aside a second later. Shrapnel had wrecked the firing mechanism.

The only other assault rifle within reach was snapped in two.

He pulled out his pistol, checked that it still appeared functional, and paced forward through the haze.

A battered form crawled across his path, trailing something dark behind it. Jacob barely heard his own shot as he took the man out of his misery.

His head swam, his nostrils filled with grit, and his lungs hacked in a persistent cough. He continued to move forward.

After passing three bodies and parts of a few more, he came across another survivor, lying on his back, half-conscious with a gut wound and one hand blown away. Jacob kicked all nearby weapons out of reach and left him. He needed prisoners to question once he could hear again.

The smoke began to clear, and the full devastation of what he had done grew apparent.

The camp was obliterated, the stack of ammo crates and the mortars had vanished. The prefabs and tents were all flat on the ground, as was every person. Bits of burning material, from the campfires and from anything combustible, were scattered all over the ravine.

Jacob made a slow turn, looking for any other survivors.

His turn ended with the sight of a rifle muzzle staring him in the face from a few paces away.

It was the rifleman who had almost killed him before, the one with a level head and frightening aim. His headscarf had been blown away from the blast, revealing a bloody face and half the hair burned away. His robes were in tatters, and blood trickled down his bare chest, but his rifle remained steady. Behind it glared a pair of eyes that reflected the fires all around them.

The man squeezed the trigger.

CHAPTER THIRTEEN

The terrorist aimed right for Jacob's head and began to squeeze the trigger.

He did not get a chance to squeeze it all the way.

Jana aimed the AK-47 she'd stolen from one of the sentries by the vehicles and fired.

The terrorist's head exploded like a melon. He fell sideways and thumped on the ground.

Jacob turned and gaped. Jana gave him a satisfied smile.

"What the hell are you doing here?" he bellowed.

"Saving you."

"What?"

"Saving you," she repeated, louder this time. Her own ears were ringing, and she had barely entered the canyon when whatever he detonated had gone off. The poor guy had been right in the middle of it all. He must be stone deaf.

"How did you get here?" he said, too loudly.

"I followed you. What do you think?"

It had been a hell of a trip. As soon as Jacob had left her tent, she had packed her gear, told one of the police officers on duty that she had received an emergency call from her sister, whose imaginary illness had been her previous excuse for a sudden disappearance, and told him that she was back in the hospital.

She then texted Brian the same thing and asked him to run the excavation until she got back.

Jana should have woken him up, but she didn't trust herself to lie convincingly to his face.

Then she had set off with one of the Jeeps, some spare Jerry cans of fuel in the back along with a rucksack of necessities, and drove east.

Jacob had mentioned that he needed to hit a base in the Béchar Province, and a look at Google Earth told her his most probable entry point across the border.

She wished she had the more accurate satellite images he'd be privy to via the CIA. Those would help her guesswork a lot.

Estimating his path and speed, she had trailed him until the sun rose and all through the following day, along busy highways and narrow back roads, through urban areas and desert wasteland, all the way to the Algerian border clear on the other side of the country.

It had been a grueling, exhausting drive, but if Jacob Snow could do it, so could Jana Peters. She was Aaron Peters's daughter, after all, so she and Jacob had been trained by the same man.

All that long day, one question had kept going around and around in her head—why was she doing this?

She didn't have a clear answer. She had followed him out of a sense of overriding instinct, a compulsion to be part of this mission. Was it because it might be connected with the attempt on her life? Except, there was a good chance that it wasn't. A sense of adventure? Maybe. A protective feeling for Jacob? A little, even though being protective of the deadliest man on the planet was more than ridiculous.

Not wanting to be left behind? That was closer to the truth. Something was going down, and she had the knowledge to help. Why should she sit on the sidelines?

Because you're not a CIA operative, and you weren't invited on this mission. You may have the knowledge to help, but you don't have the skills. This is suicidal.

She kept on driving.

At the border the next night, things got tricky. She assumed Jacob would get help from the Moroccans to infiltrate the border and elude Algerian patrols. She could rely on no such help. There were three back country roads leading to the border in that region, and the rough terrain forbade going off-road in anything less than a quad bike. So, she guessed at the most likely road and, with her lights off, tried to catch up to Jacob for the first time since she had set out to follow him.

She'd guessed right and almost gave herself away. She drove over the brow of a hill and noticed a cluster of vehicles up ahead, also with their lights off and parked behind another hill that shielded them from view of the border, which lay just beyond.

There was no checkpoint on this lonely road, only the distant lights of an Algerian army patrol passing along the desert a couple of miles ahead.

No doubt the Moroccans had an observer posted atop the hill to watch, but he was facing Algeria, not back toward Morocco, so he didn't spot Jana.

She had driven off road a little, nearly bottoming out her Jeep and making far too much noise, until she found a place she could park out of view of the road.

Then she had waited.

About an hour later, she heard several vehicles pass, heading west. Guessing them to be the Moroccans, and that they had successfully gotten Jacob across the border, she waited a few minutes and, praying they hadn't left any observers in the area, got back on the road and followed him into Algeria.

For what remained of the darkness, she was fortunate enough to have only one way to go, with flatlands bounded to the north and south by mountains. As the sun rose, she saw she had lost the trail, but an hour of zigzagging across the open landscape finally brought her within sight of a fresh set of Jeep tracks heading northeast.

She followed. A couple of times she saw a plume of dust in the distance and slowed to avoid him spotting her. There was no one else in that bleak landscape to notice. She hoped the Algerian army didn't find the tracks and decide to investigate.

Then the trail led into a rougher area complete with narrow canyons. Guessing the base was close, she had hidden her Jeep behind a heap of boulders and proceeded on foot.

That had been the worst part of the trip. She had underestimated the distance Jacob would continue to go and walked for miles in the searing sun, her water slowly diminishing. She had almost turned back when she came across his vehicle hidden in a narrow defile.

She had hidden then, too, not knowing where Jacob had set up to wait for the night.

Jana had drifted off, hidden in the shade between two large rocks, only to jerk awake hours later when Jacob passed right by her hiding place.

She had followed at a distance, sensing more than seeing or hearing the man she needed to follow.

When she got within sight of a faint campfire shining behind a collection of vehicles, she knew that she had made it.

But now what? She had no weapon other than a flare gun that her crew kept for safety reasons in all the dig vehicles, and no clear idea where Jacob or the main terrorist base was.

So, she waited for Jacob to make his move, and boy did he. Soon a narrow canyon just past the vehicles lit up with gunfire and grenade explosions.

Time to act. The sentries at the vehicles now on the alert but looking back toward the canyon, she crept forward along the darkened desert floor just as her father had taught her on those rare, precious times the government let him come home. She got to the nearest truck, opened up one of the spare fuel cans strapped to the side, and let the gasoline gush out. The racket Jacob was making masked the sound.

She retreated a decent distance and fired a flare at the gasoline puddle.

That had worked beyond her wildest imaginings. The truck detonated in a fireball, and that set off the truck parked right next to it.

A chain reaction ensued, and one by one each vehicle lit up.

The sentries were obliterated in the inferno.

All but one.

One man had been rushing back toward the ravine when the vehicles went up. Jana came across him as she made her way to help Jacob. The terrorist lay face down on the ground, gasping, his back blackened by the heat of the flames, unable to do more than let out little cries of pain, his twitching fingers the only movement his agony would allow.

Jana grabbed his gun, burnt her fingers on the metal parts, and carried it by the wooden stock as she entered the canyon.

Just in time to save his life.

Now, Jacob stared at her in wonder. Jana basked in the attention. All that training turned out to be useful.

The moment passed too quickly.

"You shouldn't be here," he snapped. "But now that you are, help me look for survivors."

That didn't take long. Most of the men were obviously dead. They only found three still alive—a man on his back missing a hand who was slipping into unconsciousness, another terrorist knocked out cold who didn't look like he'd wake up anytime soon, and a third who lay stunned with several minor wounds.

Jana bound him up with the straps taken from several assault rifles.

Jacob came storming up to her. "This has been a waste of time," he shouted, still deafened from the holocaust he had unleashed.

"What do you mean?"

"I was thinking the two foreign nationals with the group were the same as those who killed your colleague, but I just found them, or at least what's left of them. Since they're here, then The Sword of the

Righteous probably isn't involved. Damn it! I wish they had survived long enough to question."

The man she had tied up struggled at his bonds.

"This is the only person capable of answering your questions," Jana said.

"Yeah, let's drag him to a defensible position. We don't know if there may be other sentries or scouts out in the desert sneaking back on us. I didn't see any when I reconnoitered the area, but it's better to be safe."

Together they hauled the man behind the smoldering ruins of a prefab hut at the rear end of the one of the overhangs.

Jana hunkered down behind the heap of splintered wood and twisted aluminum, peering through the smoke, and looking for signs of movement in the ravine by the light of the fires scattered throughout the destroyed camp. She kept her AK-47 ready, knowing she would use it without hesitation.

Something had changed between the start of the last mission and the start of this one. She no longer feared using lethal force on those who would use it against her.

And she had learned the terrible mathematics that Jacob labored under, and her father had labored under while he was still alive—that to kill these men ended up saving lives in the long run and that not pulling the trigger made you an even worse murderer.

She had not come to terms with that grim truth, far from it, but she had learned to live with it enough that it didn't stop her from doing what she needed to do.

Her lungs filled with dust and the stench of death, the assault rifle still felt hot to her scorched hands, and her eyes blinked at the grit and cinders blowing through the air, but she knew she could do what she had to do.

Just like Jacob. He got to work on the prisoner.

"Your friends are all dead. No one is coming to save you, and no one will see you if you save yourself. Cooperate and you can go free. You could have a long life ahead of you. All you need to do is speak."

Jana glanced over her shoulder and looked at the prisoner properly for the first time. He was a young Tuareg, a lean man of the desert, and he didn't look more than twenty years old.

"I will not help you, unbeliever."

"You don't have to help me, just help yourself. We know you've recruited foreigners, French and French Canadians. Why?"

"Those from the unbelieving countries who accept the Word and wish to wage jihad are more than welcome in our ranks."

Jana looked away, shaking her head. He sounded like he was repeating something he heard from one of the radical preachers who screamed at congregations in small towns across the region, or who spewed their hate over the airwaves on pirate radio stations. She didn't think Jacob was going to get anything from this youthful subject of brainwashing.

But the CIA agent didn't give up. The case was too important not to try.

"We'll send all those Western traitors to hell," he told the Tuareg.

"They're both in paradise now."

"I mean the others."

"There are no others in Algeria, heretic. You're wasting your time."

Jana raised an eyebrow. This young man wasn't terribly bright, and he had just seen all his comrades killed and him left without entrance to Paradise. He must be rattled. Perhaps he could be manipulated.

Jacob kept at him. "How many men did you lose tonight? Thirty? Thirty-five? You're not going to be able to raid Israel now!" Jacob laughed.

"One day, God willing, we will raid the Jewish oppressor state and liberate Jerusalem and all the Holy Land!"

"Yeah, right. You know your agents in England have been traced there? We just caught them."

"If only we had agents doing such glorious work. God willing, we will one day."

"Oh, come on kid! We know all about your plan to take the Ark."

Silence.

Jana looked over her shoulder and saw the young terrorist staring at Jacob with a mixture of confusion and suspicion.

"Admit it now, and I'll let you live," Jacob said.

"Admit what?" The prisoner was now thoroughly confused.

"All right if that's the way you want it. Admit it, and I'll give you martyrdom. You seem pretty eager for that."

"Admit what?" the terrorist asked again.

It was now plain to Jana, and no doubt Jacob, too, that he wasn't shamming.

This cell of The Sword of the Righteous had nothing to do with the plan to steal or destroy the Ark of the Covenant.

The entire bloody raid had been a waste of time that they could not afford.

CHAPTER FOURTEEN

"The mercenary got killed."

Alpha One looked up from his communique.

Gamma Two stood before him in the plain concrete room of the bunker, a burly man in his younger years, in contrast to Alpha One's graying hair and compact, pantherish body. Gamma Two was head of external communications, brains as well as brawn. Enough to be trusted with The Order's contacts with the outside world, but no match for Alpha One. An endless succession of operations and chess and sparring matches in between those operations, had shown the older man to be the better in all ways.

"Who killed him?"

"Unclear. Our contacts in the police say he died from multiple gunshot wounds and grenade shrapnel, apparently from his own grenade."

"Jacob Snow?"

"He was last seen in Marrakesh, so it's possible, and he hasn't been spotted in Marrakesh since the mercenary failed. Jana has also disappeared."

Alpha One sat back and considered. The Order frequently employed freelancers to mask its own identity and intentions. While it was better to handle things yourself, secrecy was of paramount importance. The Tunisian had been a good choice, a true professional. He should have been able to handle a woman with only informal training, even if that training had come from Aaron Peters.

So, he had been intercepted, most likely by Jacob. Although he couldn't discount the possibility that another CIA agent had been involved. Jana was getting close to that organization, far too close. She had helped out on the Suez Canal operation, an operation that ironically helped The Order too since they smuggled so much of their material through that maritime channel. It was not beyond the realm of possibility that she was helping out the CIA again.

"We're trying to track them," Gamma Two said. "There's some indication that they've left Morocco together."

"Where to?"

"We're not sure yet."

Alpha One tapped his finger on his desk, lost in thought for a moment.

"Another mission? That's a bad development. She'll gain more experience in the field. She might even be taken on as a full-time civilian assistant. We can't have that. We need to grab her while she's still vulnerable."

"I still think we should go straight for Jacob, instead of pussyfooting around with secondary targets," Gamma Two growled.

Alpha One smiled. While his word was law, he encouraged subordinates to speak their mind. It provided smoother operations and was good for morale.

"And where should we go for him? We only hear about him after he's been and gone. He's like a phantom."

"Post a watchman outside the Athens field office and wait until he shows up. Yes, it could take days. Weeks. Months even. But then we could tail him to his house."

They knew that Jacob had a house somewhere on the outskirts of Athens, but they had not been able to determine where.

"That won't work. The agents at the field office would spot a watchman."

"A shopfront has just come up for rent on that street."

"Where is it in relation to the Chinese restaurant and the fruit seller?"

Both of those businesses were run by people on the CIA payroll. Gamma Two grimaced.

"All right, but how do we get Jana now that's she's disappeared with the main target?"

Alpha One gave a little shrug. "Put out feelers. Perhaps we'll catch sight of them."

"They could be anywhere in the Middle East."

"They could, and we probably won't find them, but remember that we're playing the long game, my friend. Sooner or later their mission will end, and Jana will go back to her dig, or her university, and then we can grab her. That will bring Jacob running right to us."

Gamma Two grinned. "And if we get Jacob, that will bring Aaron Peters running to us."

* * *

Jana sat scrunched as far as she could get from Jacob in the passenger's seat of his Jeep. Dawn was brightening the sky to the east, and they had left the scene of the battle behind and were making their way to where Jana had hidden her own vehicle a few miles away.

There had been no survivors of the fight at the ravine. After questioning the young terrorist, Jacob had put a bullet through his head, and then did the same with the two dying terrorists. After that, he had methodically gone around the bodies to make sure everyone was dead.

He had murdered three prisoners, two of whom weren't even conscious, and Jana hadn't even objected.

She told herself that was because he wouldn't listen. He would say that he couldn't let these men live because they would go on to kill others. They would also tell their superiors who had conducted the attack. After he had made sure everyone was dead, he had found some paint in one of the prefabs and painted the name of Al Qaeda in the Islamic Magreb in big letters on the canyon wall.

He wanted to instigate a fight between the two groups, so his killing would generate more killing.

Jana thought this cold, calculating, and cruel. At the same time, she knew it was a brilliant strategy, turning the terror groups against each other so they wouldn't have as much energy and resources to hurt innocent civilians or the Algerian government.

She felt disgusted by him because she was beginning to be like him.

If Jacob was aware of her thoughts, he gave no sign. The early dawn light shone on his weary face, bloodshot eyes in constant motion, looking for signs of movement in the landscape around them.

Jana got them to where she had hidden her Jeep and jumped out with relief. Jacob grabbed a satellite phone from the back.

"I'm going to call a general in Morocco who will get us back across the border. The Moroccan army knows the pattern of Algerian patrols and will help us slip through. That's how I got over in the first place. It's pretty impressive that you did it without help."

"I just followed you at a distance. Your army friends nearly caught me."

"Still, I'm really impressed. Thanks for saving me back there and bandaging up my leg."

"How does it feel?"

"I've had worse."

Jacob had been limping and having to keep using his leg for the accelerator and the brake must have been painful.

They looked at each other for a moment.

"I should come with you to Israel," Jana said. She didn't want to go but felt obligated. And, in a strange way that made her deeply uncomfortable, she kind of did want to go.

Jacob chuckled. "Well, if I tell you no, you'll only end up following me, so I guess I'll say yes. You made the last mission successful, and I have a feeling you'll make this one successful too. So yeah, you can come."

Jana wasn't sure how she felt about that. Relieved and terrified at the same time.

"Is your boss going to allow that?"

"I have some leeway when it comes to bringing outsiders into the team. And Wallace is a good guy. He doesn't slow things down with bureaucracy."

"I see." Part of her had been hoping that his boss would object.

Jana went to her Jeep as Jacob got on his satellite phone. It looked like they had a long journey ahead.

By the time she got her Jeep started and drove back to Jacob's side, he was hanging up the satellite phone.

"We'll meet the Moroccans at the border. They've given me a time of arrival, but I'll call in to check fifty miles east of the border to make sure the Algerian patrols haven't changed. Turn off your engine. I need to put in a call to Wallace, and I don't want him to know you're here. I'll let him believe that I picked you up in Morocco."

Jana did as she was asked. Jacob turned on the speaker option.

"I thought I'm not supposed to hear classified conversations," Jana said. She remembered him getting upset the last time she overheard one.

Jacob grinned. "What he doesn't know can't hurt us, and you need to know everything if you're going to be much help."

He put in the call. Wallace picked up.

"Hey, buddy, how's it going?" Jacob said in a cheery tone.

"A grinding amount of work and stress as usual. Where are you?"

"Still in Algeria. I took out The Sword of the Righteous base and made it look like an Al Qaeda hit. The two foreign nationals were there. A prisoner I interrogated said he had no idea what I was talking about when I asked him about the Ark, and I believe him. This is a dead end."

"I've just got some intel that a splinter group of Hamas called The Palestinian Jihad for the Liberation of Jerusalem is planning something. Get back on the Moroccan side of the border and get to Israel as soon as possible. The folks at the field office there will fill you in on the latest."

"All right. I figured this would take me to Israel sooner or later. I've never heard of The Palestinian Jihad for the Liberation of Jerusalem, and I thought I'd heard of every faction in the Middle East."

"They just formed a few months ago. They're critical of Hamas for not being more belligerent against Israel, and for not installing a harsh enough brand of Sharia law in the Palestinian Territories."

Jacob grunted. "It's not like life there is a picnic, and these idiots want to make it worse?"

"They're mostly madrasa students in the West Bank, riled up by radical clerics. Unfortunately, they've recruited a fair number of university students, too, including engineering and chemistry students."

"Bombs and bioweapons?"

"That's what we're afraid of. They haven't made any attacks yet, but our operatives say it's just a matter of time. Because of their association with learning institutions, they have contacts in the West, and there's some indication that some radicalized Western students and teachers might have joined them."

"Sounds like a good first place to look. Whoever these Westerners are who are searching for the Ark, they'd have trouble working inside Israel without local help."

"Exactly. It's still a stretch, but it's the best we have so far. We'll keep digging. Get to Israel as fast as you can. And if you feel you need some extra help with information on their supposed target, feel free to tap that archaeologist again. She was useful in the last mission."

Jacob and Jana looked at each other. Jacob got a mischievous smile. "Yeah, she might come in handy, and considering that I just saved her ass from an assassin, she owes me one."

Jana held up a finger, then lowered it.

"Well, maybe she'll get a chance to make it even," Wallace said.

Jana clapped her hands over her mouth to keep from laughing. Her anger at Jacob vanished in a feeling of camaraderie. They were in this together, and she shouldn't have any bad feelings toward him just for having to make hard decisions in a hard world.

"Right. Talk to you later, boss."

He hung up.

"Told you he was a good guy. Let's get to the border. By the time we do, Wallace will have arranged a flight for us."

They headed out across the barren, rocky plain, Jana feeling a tingle of anticipation and fear.

She had just gotten herself into a whole heap of trouble again.

CHAPTER FIFTEEN

A light industrial complex just outside Jerusalem, Israel
The next afternoon

They met with the construction company as planned. They were all tired after a long ride across the Negev, grieving the three good Aryans who had died in the fight and tense as they passed through a couple of checkpoints on the highway.

But the Jewish troops were lax. Focused as the soldiers were on searching every square inch of every vehicle driven by a Palestinian, they made only a cursory inspection of the three Land Rovers licensed to an American tour company. The guns and ANFO hidden beneath the camping gear weren't found.

Carl Bryson and his team drove through the electronic gate of the construction company, which had opened at their honk, and entered a large lot. A work building and garage stood to one side of the lot, and a forklift and a small crane were parked nearby.

A tall, blond man came out of the building to greet them. He wore a *kippah* on his head and a t-shirt emblazoned with the Israeli flag.

"What the hell?" Brett Fisher said.

"Appearances can be deceiving," Carl Bryson said with a chuckle. "He's one of us, like I told you."

"Why is he degrading himself like that?"

"Camouflage. He and his crew all got forged documents in their home countries saying they were Jewish. Birth certificates and everything. Then they immigrated using the Right of Return, a law the Israelis have saying any Jew can live in Israel."

Carl Bryson put the Land Rover in park, got out, and strode up to Ole Larsson, a dedicated Norwegian Nazi who ran Holy Land Restoration, a construction company that specialized in restoring and preserving Israel's many historic buildings. For years, he and his men had lived among the Jews, restoring synagogues, or shoring up the crumbling walls of ancient sites dating to the time of King David. Their expertise had earned them respect and renown.

Most importantly, it had earned them access.

For years, the Aryan Front had been researching the ultimate weapon, suspecting all along that it would be hidden somewhere in the Holy Land.

Now, thanks to that weakling they tortured in England, they had the last, vital clue.

And thanks to the diligent work of Ole Larsson and his two assistants, they could get into the Temple Mount.

"How did the Negev operation go?" Ole asked.

Carl made a face. "We lost three but got away clean with the ANFO."

"How much?"

Ole didn't seem affected at all about the fallen brothers. He'd been a police officer in Norway for years and didn't hurt easily.

"Way more than your requirements," Carl said.

Ole smiled. "Well, we don't know exactly what our requirements are. I gave you a high estimate."

"We got enough to blow half of the Temple Mount away."

The Norwegian's eyes glittered. "So even if we don't find it, we score a victory."

"Damn right," Gerald Hunter, the explosives expert, said as he sauntered up. "We'll blast away the Dome of the Rock and the Wailing Wall. The Jews and Muslims will blame each other for the destruction of their holy spots, and we'll have a full-on race war."

"We're going after bigger game," Carl reminded him.

"Come on, the Rod of Aaron? Get real."

Carl's hand moved a quick as a cobra's clamping around Gerald's neck.

The man froze. He was not a small man. He had been an amateur boxer and had taken martial arts training with the rest of them, but Carl was on a far, far higher level of ability.

Any other man who had taken Gerald Hunter by the throat would have immediately found himself in a tough and merciless fight, but not Carl Bryson.

"The Ark of the Covenant is there, brother, and you are lucky that you're needed on this operation, or you would be cut down for being an unbeliever."

"All I'm saying is that millions of Jews and Muslims would die in a race war," Gerald squeaked. "That's what we want, isn't it?"

The rest of the group was watching now. Some smiled, but none laughed. They didn't want to attract attention to themselves.

"A race war?" Carl snorted. "Is that as far as you can see? When we open the Ark and withdraw the Rod of Aaron, we will have a weapon far more powerful than any race war. A race war will kill millions, maybe. The Rod of Aaron will kill all of them."

Ole nodded, his eyes taking on the same fanatical gleam. The others looked away. Most agreed with the explosives expert, but they were too smart or too scared to support him.

Better to simply go along with Carl's mad plan, because when he found there were no tunnels underneath the Temple Mount, he would fly into a rage and order the entire area detonated.

Gerald would turn out to be right, and they'd get their race war.

* * *

At the CIA field office in Jerusalem, Jacob Snow met with the local director, Abraham Feinstein. An older man whose kippah didn't quite cover his bald spot, and wearing a sweater over his ample belly, Feinstein looked more like an indulgent uncle than a seasoned CIA operative, but Jacob had heard some crazy tales of his exploits in his younger years.

This man had stopped a lot of terrorist bombings, and had even convinced a Syrian general to defect and give up state secrets in exchange for a new life and new identity in the United States. That had led to a mission to take out a Syrian bioweapons plant, setting the program back at least ten years.

Now, Jacob listened as Feinstein gave him the rundown on The Palestinian Jihad for the Liberation of Jerusalem.

"We've been working with Mossad on this. The Israeli secret service is being very forthcoming because they've linked at least three American radicals to the group. So, we've been tracing these guys on our end and in return, Mossad has kept us in the loop. I'll get to the Americans in a minute. First let's talk about the Palestinians. It appears that before making a formal break from Hamas, a group of professors and students began to meet informally. They realized that together they knew a fair number of foreigners sympathetic to the cause and began to cultivate them."

Jacob nodded. Israel was a magnet for foreign radicals for both sides. It was a major headache for the Israeli government.

"So, who are these Americans?"

Feinstein handed over a dossier. “Two students and a professor. The students are both taking Islamic Studies at Palestine Ahliya University in Bethlehem. The professor teaches Political Science at Eastern Illinois University and is over here on sabbatical.”

Jacob frowned as he flipped through the dossier. One of the students was some nineteen-year-old from the suburbs of Boston now sporting Islamic dress, a skullcap, and a wispy beard. He looked more Muslim than most Muslims in Palestine. Dumb kid. That kind of radical chic might get him killed. The other student, also nineteen, was from Little Rock, had joined the Nation of Islam in his early teens before leaving them a couple of years later to join a radical mosque run by a Palestinian preacher in his hometown. He’d gotten a scholarship from the mosque to come to Palestine.

The professor was an older white guy with a long history of Marxist writings that led him to espouse support for various nationalistic movements from the Basques to Northern Ireland to Palestine. There was no indication that he was actually a Muslim, merely a fellow traveler.

Could these be some of the killers? They were older or younger than Jacob had pictured them, although that didn’t mean they weren’t capable of violence.

“Are there any other foreigners in their ranks?” Jacob asked.

“Not that we know of, but we know very little. The group is so new that we haven’t been able to infiltrate it yet. Everything we know is second hand based on monitoring we did on these people before they founded The Palestinian Jihad for the Liberation of Jerusalem.”

“What’s Hamas doing about them?”

“Nothing. The group hasn’t made a move yet. I’m sure Hamas is talking to them, trying to bring them back in the fold, but since they haven’t launched any attacks, they don’t really need to be brought to heel.”

Jacob grunted. “And if they do launch an attack, that fits in with Hamas’s long-term strategy. They get Israeli blood and no accountability.”

“Exactly. I can’t count how many times I’ve seen them pull that trick.”

“You don’t think they’d be dumb enough to attack Hamas targets, do you?” It had happened with other splinter groups.

“I don’t think so. From what we know about the leadership, they’re obsessed with killing Jews. They might criticize Hamas for not being militant enough, but they would want to establish their reputation by hitting Israeli targets first."

"Do they have any history or archaeology students or professors among them?"

"A couple. Why?"

"I got some intel that the killers I'm after want to find the Ark of the Covenant."

Feinstein snickered. "That's dumb even by terrorist standards."

"Sure, but their quest is leaving a trail of blood."

"I don't recall any of the members having any research interests like that, but I'll look into it. Of course, there are lots of religious studies students in that crowd, and they'd be familiar with the stories surrounding the Ark."

"Could be," Jacob mused.

That Tuareg kid he'd interrogated had barely heard of the thing. Living in some dusty desert village, his only education had been what he'd learned in the *madrasa* or the terrorist training camp. Jacob bet the guy was barely literate. The Palestinian population were a lot more sophisticated, mostly urban and with easy access to the Internet and at least some formal education. A lot more likely to know the lore of one of the holiest objects in the region's history.

"You're not convinced these are the guys you're looking for," Feinstein said.

"No. But it's not like I have a whole lot of leads," he replied, still flipping through the dossier.

"Well, maybe you'll strike it lucky this evening."

Jacob looked up. "What do you mean?"

"Mossad has decided to nip them in the bud, send a warning to anyone else who wants to break away from Hamas. While Hamas is the main threat, it's a predictable threat. We don't want to add to the chaos by having more groups in the mix. The government already has its hands full with the Sabireen Movement, the Army of Islam, the Palestinian Islamic Jihad . . ." Feinstein's sentence trailed off into a shrug. They both knew the list of radical groups, and it was a long one.

Jacob grimaced. Palestine was like a Petrie dish for radicals. Groups were always appearing, merging, and splitting.

"But this will provoke a response," he said.

"A predictable response. Hamas will launch a few rockets into Israel that probably won't hit anything, and the Israelis will make some drone strikes on suspected bomb-making facilities. It will all die down in a week."

Feinstein made it sound routine, almost boring.

"So, you want in?" Feinstein asked.

"Yeah, I want in."

"This is supposed to be an Israeli-only operation. We don't want Hamas thinking the United States is a legitimate target. You're going to be wearing an Israeli Defense Forces uniform and body armor. Also, let's add another layer of disguise."

Feinstein reached under his sweater and pulled a gold chain over his head. At the end dangled a gold Star of David.

"You want me to pretend to be Jewish?"

Feinstein grinned. "Your dossier says you're circumcised. You're halfway there already."

"I like bacon."

"Nobody's perfect," Feinstein said, holding out the chain.

Jacob took the chain and put it on.

"It will give you luck," the field office director told him. "I've worn that on more missions than I can count and have loaned it out to agents too. I'll hook you up with the IDF and Mossad team, and they'll prep you. Good luck. You're striking one for the good guys tonight."

CHAPTER SIXTEEN

Jacob sat on an uncomfortable metal bench in the back of a van, pressed in by IDF soldiers to either side.

The van could comfortably hold six men. There were ten in the back, eight men and two women in Kevlar and helmets, complete with Galil assault rifles, sidearms, and grenades. Two more sat up front. Jacob was similarly equipped, Feinstein's Star of David hanging over the front of his Kevlar vest. The air was stifling, and Jacob could barely move. Plus, one of these bastards had farted. He wished he knew who it was. A bit of friendly fire would teach them a lesson.

An unmarked car with tinted windows and four more men, which had entered Palestinian territory hours before, would rendezvous with them.

They were driving through a suburb of Bethlehem, a run-down collection of concrete houses and apartment blocks that the pilgrims and tourists never saw.

They'd passed through Palestinian Authority checkpoints at the border without permission, as the IDF often did when going into Palestinian territory in search of terrorists. The main column, including a couple of armored personnel carriers, had peeled off to enter downtown Bethlehem. They were the distraction. They'd drive around, startling the residents out for evening strolls and attracting lots of attention, while this unmarked van headed for the real target. A couple of drones flew as scouts high overhead, invisible in the night.

Jacob tried to clear his mind, ease the tension before the fight kicked off. Waiting was always the worst part. He tried not to think about the ache of his leg wound and how that might slow him down at a critical moment.

Instead, he found himself thinking about Jana, safe in a Jerusalem hotel, grumbling about not being allowed along on the raid. She'd grumble more if he solved all this by himself. Still, it was good to have her along. He'd missed her.

The unit commander, Captain Mizrahi, an olive-skinned man with brown eyes and a jagged scar on his chin, murmured into his earpiece and then announced, "Two minutes. We pile out the moment we stop.

You all know your posts. We do this quick, and we do this clean. Each suspect gets a chance to surrender. One chance. If they don't, shoot to kill."

This was said in Hebrew. Captain Mizrahi did not repeat it in English. He already knew the CIA operative in his ranks spoke his language. He didn't know why Jacob was there and didn't ask. He was a soldier, and he followed orders.

The van slowed, then screeched to a halt.

The man closest to the back door flung it open, and the soldiers filed out in rapid succession.

Jacob found himself on a poorly lit street. The backup car was parked right in front of their van. A row of five-story apartment buildings rose to one side. The compound they needed to hit was on the other side. The drones had shown a ten-foot-high concrete wall topped with razor wire. There were three buildings inside: one two-story and the others were one-story.

The street was abandoned. As soon as the unmarked and windowless van had stopped, the street-savvy Palestinians, born and raised in one of the most politically tense regions in the world, had immediately figured out what was about to go down and had made themselves scarce. The last windows slammed shut just as Jacob hopped out of the van.

Gripping his Galil, he rushed over to the iron gate just as the biggest member of the team, a Sephardi Jew from Morocco who looked like his mother had added steroids to his couscous, slammed a handheld steel battering ram against the lock.

The gate sprang open. The soldiers swarmed in.

Jacob came in the middle. His role was to move right and, with six others from the team, take the main building. The other six from the van and the four guys from the car would take the two smaller buildings and secure the gate and street.

He left them to it and focused on what was in front of him, his gaze darting to every window, the rooftop, and the edges of the building. Shouts behind him in Hebrew and Arabic told him the section dealing with one of the smaller buildings had made contact.

His section came to the front door of the building. All the ground floor shutters were shut tight. Dim light shone in the upper windows through curtains of dark green.

One of the IDF soldiers clamped a magnetic bomb about the size of a baseball against the lock and everyone edged away, hugging the wall.

A favorite terrorist trick was to booby trap the front door, so when you smash it in you get blown to pieces. The drones had checked that the front gate wasn't trapped but couldn't check the inside of the buildings.

The bomb exploded with a loud bang. The door swung open and one of the IDF soldiers shouted through a megaphone in Arabic, "Get down on the floor with your hands behind your heads. You are all under arrest."

No one thought that would actually work. But that was how the IDF rolled. You got one chance. After that, the ass kicking began.

"Go! Go! Go!" Captain Mizrahi shouted, rushing through the door and leading from the front as Israeli officers inevitably did.

Good for morale, bad for the officers. Captain Mizrahi flew back as he took a shotgun blast to the chest, the Kevlar saving him except for a few pellets that tore into his cheek.

A female soldier tossed a flash bang inside and once again everyone hugged the wall.

It detonated a moment later with a flash and an ear-splitting thud. Jacob and the Moroccan ducked around the corner, assault rifles leveled. They saw a narrow front hall that turned to the right, a common feature in Middle Eastern homes to keep the interior out of view. A man lay stunned on the ground, blood trickling out of his ears. His shotgun lay beside him. The Moroccan cut ahead of Jacob, kicked the shotgun behind him, and swiveled to the right, firing two shots inside.

Jacob came right behind him and into a large living room where a young Palestinian was gasping his last breath on the floor, a pistol lying nearby. An open doorway led to a hallway and a staircase leading up. On the other side of the room, a door slammed. Jacob put a three-round burst through the door, aiming low to incapacitate instead of kill.

He rushed across the room at an angle to avoid any return fire through the door. None came.

His colleagues were getting heat trying to get up that staircase, though. Gunshots rose in tempo behind him.

Jacob left them to their job and focused on his. A female soldier had joined him. He kicked open the door, and the woman fired a burst even before they saw what was on the other side. She did not aim low.

She didn't hit anything, either. They saw a kitchen with a pot of soup that was leaking onto the floor thanks to a fresh bullet hole, and a closed door on the far end.

Jacob did a quick mental assessment of the drone footage he'd seen of this place earlier. There wasn't much room left on this side of the building. The door probably led to a pantry.

"You're trapped!" Jacob shouted in Arabic, keeping under cover of the doorway as the female soldier did the same. "Come out with your hands up!"

"I . . . I surrender!" came a male voice from within.

"Come out now, or I'll fire!" Jacob said.

The door creaked open. Beyond it, they saw a small pantry with shelves stocked with cans, bags of rice, and jugs of cooking oil. A stocky older man in white robes that matched the beard fringing his face stood there, hands trembling above his head.

"Step out," Jacob ordered.

He came out. Suspicion rose in Jacob's gut. The man's hands might be shaking, but his step was firm and his eyes narrow.

This man wasn't afraid at all.

The female IDF soldier slung her assault rifle and stepped forward, holding a pair of handcuffs.

"Watch this one," Jacob warned.

Just as she got within reach, the man dove for a butcher knife on the counter. The move put the soldier between Jacob and the target, ruining his shot.

It didn't matter. Just as he grabbed the knife, the woman kicked him in the knee, grabbed his wrist as he staggered, and got him in an armlock, his arm twisted painfully behind his back. Another kick took him to the ground, where she gave him three kidney punches in rapid succession, retrieved the handcuffs, and cuffed him.

"Damn," Jacob said. "You should meet my partner. You two would get along like a house on fire."

The woman grinned at him. "Is your partner as cute as you?"

"Cuter."

The firing had died down. Leaving the soldier with her prisoner, Jacob rushed out to see what was going on.

No one alive remained in the living room, so he rushed upstairs to find a dead terrorist at the top, still clutching a battered old Kalashnikov. He recognized him as the young African American student. A twist in Jacob's gut made him pause for a moment. He hated seeing dead Americans, even when they had turned traitor.

Moving beyond the staircase, he came to a hallway leading off to several bedrooms. The American professor lay on the floor, gut shot being treated by an IDF soldier. Two Palestinians were cuffed and lying face down on the floor.

"Any explosives?" he asked no one in particular.

"None yet," one of the IDF men replied. "We'll do a full search once we've cleared the compound."

Cursing, Jacob rushed downstairs and outside to find Captain Mizrahi giving orders to some of his men, ignoring the blood streaming down his face.

"We need to search for explosives," Jacob said.

"We already found them," the captain said, his speech somewhat slurred and blood coming out of his mouth. Jacob guessed his tongue had been sliced. "That building over there."

He pointed to the smallest of the three buildings in the compound, one that looked like a three-car garage.

The first clue that it wasn't was the fact that a couple of cars were parked outside it and not inside. Jacob went over.

One of the doors had been pulled open, and he found a large laboratory inside. There was an assortment of chemistry equipment on several tables. A couple hundred bags of fertilizer and several barrels of diesel fuel, enough to make a heavy-duty truck bomb, were stacked to one side. Three men—two Palestinians and the white American student—sat cross-legged on the ground, hands bound behind their backs. A glowering IDF soldier stood over them, his Galil trained on them. A couple more IDF soldiers searched the place.

Jacob crouched down in front of the American, who kept his head down, a look of defeat stamped on his face. Jacob grabbed his poor attempt at a beard and tugged on it until the idiot looked up at him.

"Where's the ANFO?" he asked in English.

The kid looked at him in confusion.

"The ANFO, the pink pellets. An explosive. Where is it?"

"Fuck off, unbeliever."

"You got it from the Bedouin. Where is it?"

"Why didn't you martyr me?" he asked, his voice cracking and tears brimming in his eyes.

Jacob resisted the urge to slap him. It wouldn't do any good. The kid didn't know anything. He stood.

"Has anyone found any ANFO in here?" he asked the room. The soldiers shook their heads.

Jacob ground his teeth.

No ANFO. He should have known it wouldn't be so easy.

He looked around, at a loss. Could it be hidden somewhere else? Buried maybe, or in another building?

But Mossad said this was the new group's only compound, and why bury it when they had a bomb making lab chock full of incriminating substances?

His gut told him this was another dead end.

Jacob stormed out of the garage and went up to Captain Mizrahi, who still hadn't bothered to staunch the wound to his face.

"Looks like a dead end as far as my mission is concerned," he told the officer.

"Sorry about that. At least we snuffed out a terror cell." Captain Mizrahi spat a gob of blood on the ground.

"Now that the compound is secure, may I have permission to go to the van and make a call? My partner is doing some research on this. Maybe she's turned up something."

Before he had left for briefing that afternoon, Jana had told him she'd delve into some of Jerusalem's famous archives.

"Granted. Good work on this, my friend. Go have a beer for me. Looks like I'll be here all night."

"Will do."

Jacob went out, past a guard at the gate and two more in the street.

Just as he did, one of the reconnaissance drones hovering far overhead started blaring a siren and blinking a red light.

A warning. Incoming hostiles.

He went to one knee, looked left and right, and saw no one. The drone swerved to the left to indicate direction and just as Jacob looked that way three Palestinians came running around the corner.

Two carried Kalashnikovs and a third had an old revolver.

"Jihad!" one shouted.

The guards at the vehicles took out one of the guys wielding an assault rifle within a second of him appearing, before having to duck for cover as the second one sprayed at them using full auto.

The guy with the revolver fired at Jacob.

Jacob fired at the same instant.

Both hit.

CHAPTER SEVENTEEN

Jacob knew only blackness. No sight, no hearing, no sensation.

Gradually, one by one, those things began to return.

First, a buzzing in his ears. Then, a tightness in his chest.

The buzzing resolved into distant, muted shouts, interrupted by the sharp crack of gunshots growing louder and louder.

The tightness grew and turned into pain.

Sight came next, blurred patches of light and darkness that slowly sharpened into a night sky, a streetlight, and the tops of buildings.

Jacob lay on his back in the middle of the street. The firing died away. He tried to remember what was going on and how he had gotten in this position, but his thoughts came slow and muddled.

A female face blotted out the streetlight. He couldn't discern the features, haloed as it was by the light.

"Jana?"

The woman knelt down, and her face resolved into that of a stranger wearing the uniform of the IDF.

"Whoever Jana is, she'll be glad you wore your Kevlar tonight."

"Kevlar?" Jacob blearily raised his head. The woman put a hand behind it to support it.

He looked down at his chest and saw the tail end of a bullet sticking out of his body armor.

"How do you feel?" the woman asked. She was speaking in English and a good thing too. Jacob didn't think he could handle Hebrew right now.

"Like an elephant stomped on my chest."

"More like a .45 bullet. They're all down now. Let's get you on your feet and into the van."

"Good idea."

The soldier hauled him up. Jacob looked around. The man who had tagged him lay on his back, his clothing soaked in blood. His two companions were dead too. A soldier was checking them while some others aimed their guns at every nearby rooftop and street corner.

"Did I get him?" Jacob asked.

"You, me, and a couple of other soldiers," the woman said as she led him to the van.

"I haven't been a soldier for a long time," he whispered, remembering Afghanistan.

"You're still a soldier."

"Yeah. Maybe." His soldiering days didn't bring back good memories, only shameful ones.

He found that he was limping more than before. His calf hurt from that frag wound he got in Algeria. He must have twisted his leg as he fell.

"Were those guys in the terror cell? They came from outside."

"Not sure yet. They might have just been neighbors who decided to get in on the action. It happens sometimes. Actually, it happens a lot."

The rumble of engines caught Jacob's attention.

"That's our backup," the soldier said. "The original column that drove off as a distraction."

She got him in the back of the van, closed the door, and started working the straps on his body armor.

"Hey," Jacob protested. "We're still in a combat situation."

"Not you. The area is all but clear, we got a full team, and heavy backup is only a block away. Plus, this van is reinforced. Nothing short of an RPG is going to get through it. I need to take a look at your chest."

She got the Kevlar off and lifted up his shirt. Like a lot of Israeli women, she was a looker, and Jacob didn't mind her leaning in closer and touching his chest with fingers that had suddenly become soft and delicate.

"Just a bad bruise, I think. How does it feel to breathe?"

"A surprising ability, considering that I thought I was dead a couple of minutes ago."

She grinned. "I mean does it hurt to breathe?"

"Not really. I don't have a fractured rib or sternum if that's what you're worried about."

She looked down. "I'm more worried about that."

He put his hands over his lap. "Sorry. Oh wait, you mean my leg."

She looked at him. "What did you think I meant?"

"Um, nothing."

She rolled up his pants leg to reveal a bloodied bandage. "Where did you that, or am I not allowed to ask?"

"You're not allowed to ask."

She looked up at him and smiled. "You're an interesting man, whatever your name is. I noticed you never told us. Whoever that Jana is, she's a lucky woman."

* * *

Jana got back to her hotel room, her eyes bleary and her neck cramped from poring over rare documents in the Israeli state archives. Her academic connections had gotten her access, and a call from Jacob's superiors had kept the archives open way past closing time.

That had given her the time to find what she needed, or at least she thought so.

Jana ordered some room service because she was too tired to go out and took a shower while she waited.

She was just getting dressed when there was a knock at her door.

"Who is it?" she called, keeping out of the line of sight of the door.

Her father had told her never to look through the peephole because anyone outside would see the pinpoint of light darken and know exactly where you were. It was also better to keep away from the door entirely in case someone decided to take a blind shot through it.

Just two of the countless pieces of advice Aaron Peters had given his daughter, advice she never thought she'd need in the real world.

All that advice was coming in handy now.

"It's me," Jacob replied.

Jana felt a little silly until she remembered what Dad had told her.

"Nine times out of ten, or ninety-nine times out of a hundred, your caution won't be needed. Keep doing it for the time it is."

Jana opened the door. Jacob limped in, rubbing his chest, his face drawn with pain.

"What happened?"

"Took a bullet in my body armor. Knocked the wind out of me and gave me the mother of all bruises."

"Oh my God! Let me see."

Without thinking, she pulled up his shirt and saw a livid bruise dead center on his chest. A man walked by in the hallway, glanced in, and snickered.

Jacob pulled down his shirt and closed the door. "Would you mind not stripping me in front of the other guests? This is a decent hotel."

"That bullet would have gone straight through your heart!"

"Keep your voice down too. It's no big deal."

"No big deal? You could have been killed."

"I can't even count the number of times I could have been killed in the past few years," Jacob said, sitting down on the bed.

"Why are you limping?"

"Strained that leg wound during the fight."

"Let me look at it."

"A soldier looked at it. The IDF all know how to do field dressings. I'm fine."

"Stop saying you're fine when you're not," Jana said, sitting down next to him.

She sat close. Only to examine his wound, of course. She tried to pull up his pants leg and he tugged it down.

"Nothing to see but a fresh bandage courtesy of the Israeli government."

"Are you sure you're all right?"

Jacob gave her a crooked smile. "I'm sure I'm not, but why are you so concerned all of a sudden?"

Suddenly, Jana felt self-conscious and looked away. "Well, I don't want to see you hurt, and we have a mission to accomplish. We can't have you out of the action."

Jacob reached for her as if to put a reassuring hand on hers, got halfway, and pulled his hand back.

"I've had this happen before. This one was a bit rougher than most, slammed me down on the pavement so hard I actually got knocked out for a second." When Jana gave him a stricken look, he hurried to add, "Only for a second, though. A good night's sleep and I should be all right."

Silence settled between them. Jana jerked as another knock sounded on the door.

"Who is it?" she asked, moving out of the line of sight. Jacob did the same.

"Room service."

Jacob shot her a questioning look, and she nodded. He went over to the door, pulling out his pistol from beneath his vest and keeping out of sight behind the doorjamb. He opened it a crack.

How can he be accustomed to this life? Jana wondered. *And how am I going to get accustomed to it?*

Wait, do I have to? There's not going to be another mission after this one, is there?

Jacob visibly relaxed, returned his gun into the shoulder holster under his vest, took the chain off, and let in a bellboy pushing a cart on which were set a couple of covered plates. Jana took off the covers and found the pasta, soup, and dessert she'd ordered. Her stomach rumbled.

Jacob's stomach rumbled even louder. He gave the bellboy a generous tip, locked and chained the door behind him, and sat down to start eating Jana's dinner.

"Um, hello?"

"What?" Jacob asked around a mouthful of spaghetti.

"You're eating my dinner!"

"I was just in a firefight. I'm hungry."

Jacob reached for the soup. Jana grabbed it first. "Stop. I'm hungry too."

"All you did was read in a library. I did physical labor," he said, still shoveling food in his mouth.

"If you think you're being cute, you're wrong. You're being selfish and annoying."

"One of the IDF soldiers said I was cute."

"Go eat his dinner then."

"Hers."

Jana frowned. "Whatever. You still haven't told me if you discovered anything on the raid."

"You never gave me a chance. You were all heartbroken over me getting a little bruise."

"I stopped being heartbroken when you stole my dinner," she said, starting on her soup and hovering close to the pie in case he got any ideas. "So, did you find anything?"

"We didn't find any ANFO, but we did find a bomb-making lab. Using fertilizer. The most inefficient way to make a bomb. Requires a huge amount of fertilizer and you end up with something you can't smuggle. I'm guessing they were going to load a vehicle and drive it against a checkpoint. I questioned a suspect and came up with nothing."

"Do you think they have nothing to do with it?"

"That's what my gut tells me. The IDF will work on them and investigate the area. Probably bust into a few more houses of people related to the group. I'm not optimistic, though."

That made Jana feel oddly satisfied. While, of course, she wanted the terrorists stopped as soon as possible, she also wanted to be part of accomplishing that. Coming all this way only to have Jacob solve the case by himself would have been a letdown.

So, it was with some pride that she told him what she'd been doing all afternoon and evening. "I've been at the archives, and I've found some scraps of information that might prove useful."

The interest Jacob showed made her feel even better. She went on, "I came across a couple of texts by medieval rabbis who place the Ark of the Covenant in tunnels underneath the Temple Mount, or more precisely, a hidden chamber in the original temple of Solomon."

"I thought the Romans destroyed that temple."

"No, the Babylonians did, and a new temple was built on its foundations. It was the Second Temple that the Romans destroyed and only partially. The Western Wall remains, as you know, so scholars think that the temple was basically gutted and then filled in with soil and rubble, leaving it level with the rest of the hill. Part of the hill is a natural eminence, you see. The power of God, and some thick masonry foundations, kept the Romans from finding the Ark or destroying it."

"Interesting. So, our jet-setting nutcases might try to dig in there and find it?"

"They might."

"Then what's the ANFO for? Blast mining?"

"I don't think so. This has all the hallmarks of religious zealots. They wouldn't want to damage such a holy site. I was on a dig once in Israel working on a Roman military camp in the Gaza Strip that happened to be right next to a Jewish cemetery, and a group of ultra-Orthodox Jews threw stones at us for disturbing the dead."

"Well, if you were digging up graves . . ."

"We weren't, we were merely digging next to the graves. That was bad enough. Plus, we got stones thrown at us by Palestinians for driving through their settlement to get to the site."

Jacob snorted. "Such a fine patch of real estate we got here. But I see your point. There are a lot of seriously protective people in these parts who don't want any of their sacred sites touched. The foreigners who come here are often even worse. And I think you're right. It's got to be some brand of religious fundamentalists. Who else would believe they could actually find the Ark of the Covenant?"

"There's more. I also found—"

A knock on the door made her heart freeze. Jacob glanced at her, a silent question on his face.

She shook her head. She hadn't ordered any more room service, and she wasn't expecting visitors.

CHAPTER EIGHTEEN

Jana hung back, her heart beating fast as Jacob approached the door.

"Who is it?" he called out.

"Tamar," a woman's voice said.

"Who?"

"With the IDF. I brought you to the van and bandaged your leg."

"Oh!" Jacob opened the door a crack, and then opened it the rest of the way to reveal a short, but strong-looking, woman in uniform with a Galil slung across her back. Jana couldn't help but notice that she was younger and more attractive than she was. Olive skin and eyes. Brown hair with blonde highlights. She even managed to look good in fatigues.

Tamar looked right at her. "You must be Jana."

"How did you know that?" Jana asked.

Jacob looked uncomfortable. It was hard to tell because he was so tanned, but Jana could have sworn that he was blushing. "How did you find us?" he asked.

"Police database. I searched for an American named Jana staying in a hotel in Jerusalem."

"Oh. Right. Um, what's up?"

"You dropped this." Tamar held out her hand and opened it. She held a gold Star of David and a snapped chain.

"Feinstein's chain!" Jacob said, taking it. "Thanks, with everything that happened I completely forgot about this. Looks like the bullet snapped the chain."

"It saved you."

"The Kevlar did that. The metal is too thin to have stopped a bullet."

Tamar smiled. "I wasn't talking about the metal." The soldier turned back to Jana. "Take good care of him. He's a bit of a disaster."

"Don't I know it."

Tamar laughed, gave them a friendly wave, and left.

Jacob closed the door and sat back on the bed, staring at the chain. "Looks like I owe Feinstein a new chain."

"Who's Feinstein?"

"CIA station director. He gave me this for luck." Jacob stared at the chain for a minute longer.

"So, Tamar is the woman who said you were cute?"

"No, that was another female soldier," he said with a grin.

"Well, maybe you should get your Israeli girlfriends to help you with the mission."

"Can't. It's classified. I could tell them, but then I would have to kill them. Hard to get a second date after that."

"You're a real comedian."

"Aren't I awesome? But back to work. You were going to tell me something."

Jana took a deep breath, decided not to slap him, and said, "I found some old texts describing how the Ark was hidden in a secret chamber built by King Solomon because he foresaw a disaster that would befall Israel."

"The destruction of the Temple by the Romans?"

"Exactly. The Rod of Aaron, some anointing oil, and a vial of the manna that sustained the Hebrews during their forty years in the wilderness were placed inside the Ark. I got to looking into the lore of Aaron's Rod and found some things that make me think that whoever is searching for the Ark may be more interested in the rod."

"Why?"

"There are only two canonical miracles connected with Aaron's rod, which was basically a walking staff and symbol of authority. Aaron was the elder brother of Moses, and a prophet and high priest in his own right, so his rod is an important relic. In one miracle, he's brought before Pharaoh and commanded to perform a miracle. He threw down his rod, and it turned into a serpent. When the Egyptian priests threw down their rods, they also turned into snakes. Then they mocked him as not being any more powerful than they were, at which point Aaron's serpent ate all the other serpents."

"Nice one."

"The other miracle came when he set it in the ground to represent the tribe of Levi, and it bloomed. This symbolized the Levite's role as the priestly class, the Kohanim."

"OK, but I don't see how this would be more important than the Ark."

"Not according to the canonical writings, no, but I found some little-known fragments of early Jewish Apocrypha that attribute even greater powers to Aaron's rod. One says that the rod was actually what brought forth the plagues of Egypt that convinced Pharaoh to let the Hebrew people go—the pestilence, wild animals, and the deaths of the firstborn sons."

"I thought God brought that down on Egypt."

"That's what made it into the Old Testament, but there are many noncanonical writings that didn't make it in and are often only known through one-of-a-kind fragments found during the course of excavations. Many haven't been published. There are so many, and they're often difficult to translate, and there are so few professional translators."

"So how would our religious zealots even know about them?"

Jana shrugged. "It's all there to see in the archives. If I could find them, so could they."

"Yeah, but you're fluent in ancient Hebrew."

"This is Israel. A lot of people are fluent in ancient Hebrew."

"So, are you saying they might want it as a weapon?"

"Could be."

"That's crazy."

Jana nodded. "I think these people are crazy."

"It doesn't bring us any closer to finding out who they are."

"No, but we know where they're going. Tomorrow, first thing, we need to go to the Temple Mount when it opens and take a look around."

* * *

"We have to wear this Jewish crap?" Brett Fisher complained.

"You're going to wear it and you're going to play the part," Carl Bryson said.

The entire crew stood in the workroom of Ole's company bright and early the next morning. It was time to get going. The Temple Mount would open in an hour and a half. They, as a work crew, were allowed in an hour early to set up before the crowds got in the way.

Brett put on his kippah with obvious distaste, muttering every swear word in the book. The others hesitated to put on their Jewish religious headwear too.

For once, Carl didn't get angry at his men for questioning his orders. Asking good Aryans to pretend to be Jews was the worst of all insults. He would never have issued this order if it hadn't been necessary.

Grimacing, he put on his own. A couple of his men snickered. He didn't mind. He really did look ridiculous.

The ends justify the means, he reminded himself.

"All right, does everyone remember the Hebrew we learned?" he asked the group.

The men nodded.

"Let's make sure," Ole said. He ran through some quick words and phrases with each man, correcting them here and there.

Not too many times, though. The men had applied themselves to this distasteful task well.

"Right," the Norwegian said once he finished the pop quiz. "Now remember, let me and my crew do all the talking since we're familiar faces and we're all fluent. If someone talks to you, tell them you're a recent immigrant coming back thanks to the Right of Return. You won't be expected to be fluent in Hebrew yet. I've actually employed several real Jewish newcomers in order gain a reputation for that. I even put it in my help wanted ads."

Brett curled his lip. "You gave money to Jews?"

Ole looked at him. "They'll get what's coming to them."

The demolitions expert smiled back at his colleague. "Yeah, you and I will make sure of that."

Carl clapped his hands. "All right, folks, let's get to it."

The men donned reflective vests and hard hats—Brett muttering that he didn't need the kippah if the hard hat was hiding it—and piled into trucks already loaded with construction and surveying gear. Carl and Ole took the lead truck.

As they drove into Jerusalem, they passed through the usual checkpoints of concrete barriers and stern-faced IDF soldiers, now on higher alert thanks to some raid into the Palestinian Territories the previous night. But like with the tour company buses, Ole's Holy Land Restoration vehicles were a familiar sight on this route and the soldiers waved them through.

Carl let out a breath of relief as they got through the last checkpoint. "No sweat," he said, trying to sound more confident than he was.

"Who would expect a group of Nazis to own a business in Israel?" Ole said with a smile.

Both men laughed, but each could hear the tension. The laughter was a little too quick, a little too loud.

Because the chances of any of them getting out alive were very, very slim.

First, they had to get through the heavy cordon of guards at the Temple Mount without any of them finding the ANFO hidden inside their tubes of scaffolding. Then they had to set up the bombs without the guards realizing what was happening. And they had to do that in an hour, with no crowds to mask their movements.

Then, and only then, could they set forth their plan.

And if everything went well, they'd uncover a secret that had been hidden under the Temple Mount for more than two thousand years.

CHAPTER NINETEEN

Jana felt a prickle of awe as they climbed the narrow street up to the entrance of the Temple Mount. She had been here many times before, initially as an undergraduate on one of her first overseas digs, then several more times when conferences or excavations of her own brought her to the Holy Land.

She had always found Jerusalem an electric place, full of history and tradition and on edge from religious tensions whose origins stretched back millennia.

Unlike many of Jerusalem's famous sights—the Church of the Holy Sepulchre and the Via Dolorosa, the Tower of David and the Mount of Olives—she found that she came back here again and again. She had seen all those other places, of course, some of them several times, but only the Temple Mount drew her back any time she visited the city.

Its commanding position overlooking the old city, its brilliant Islamic architecture, and its storied past made it impossible to resist.

They ascended past narrow shopfronts set into low stone buildings. The owners—Muslim, Christian, and Jewish—were just rolling up their metal shutters. The windows behind revealed displays of rosaries, prayer books, saints' icons, and other religious items for all three major religions. The crowds would start coming in half an hour, and the shop owners wanted to be ready.

Jana smiled. She had read travel accounts from the Middle Ages where pilgrims complained of the holy city being full of shops like this, whose owners would grab at you and try to drag you inside. Even if you avoided them, self-appointed guides would follow you everywhere, pestering you to hire them.

It had been much the same when she had first come here in the nineties, but the Israeli government had cracked down on that and things were now much more relaxed. The shops remained, however. The selling of religion as a commodity and a political tool was just as much a part of Jerusalem's history as anything else.

They came to the entrance, an open stone arch through a medieval stone wall. Blue, metal barriers were set up to corral the crowd, and even at this early hour, there were already several dozen people patiently waiting. An American woman was leading a small group in a very loud evangelical prayer, while next to them an Orthodox Jew rocked back and forth as he read the Torah to himself, completely ignoring the ruckus.

Several heavily armed police officers stood by the arch—complete with Kevlar, helmets, and assault rifles—ready for trouble. They often got it. The medieval gate itself was fitted with a metal barrier and bulletproof guardhouse. To her surprise, she saw the gate was already open.

She checked her watch. No, it was still half an hour before opening.

They cut through the line and went to the front. Jacob walked ahead of her. She noticed that he was still limping.

"We open in half an hour," a guard told him in English. "Please wait in line."

"I'm Jacob Snow. The chief of police called about me."

The cop pulled out a phone, opened up a text with a few lines of Hebrew and a photo of Jacob. He held it up and compared the two. Then he nodded, turned to Jana, and swiped his phone to look at something Jana couldn't see. He looked from Jana to the phone and back again, then nodded.

Wait. The CIA has a photo of me, and they shared it with the Israelis?

"Come," he said, taking them to the gate.

In Hebrew, Jacob said in a low voice. "I'm carrying. A 9-mm in a shoulder holster under my vest."

"You will have to leave it."

They came to the guardhouse, where a man stood behind bulletproof glass. Three more policemen stood arrayed across the entrance to the Temple Mount, forming a wall of muscle, Kevlar, and deadly weaponry.

"I need it," Jacob objected. "I have a permit signed by the chief of police."

"That doesn't apply here."

"If you call the chief, I'm sure—"

"That doesn't apply here. No one other than Israeli police and the IDF are allowed weapons on the Temple Mount. Please hand it over."

Jacob and the guard stared at each other for a moment. It quickly became obvious that the guard would not budge. He had his orders, and those orders were cast in iron.

To Jacob's credit, he didn't bluster or complain like many men would. Instead, he shrugged in a slightly exaggerated way to show his disapproval and opened his vest. The guard reached in and removed the pistol. Then he patted Jacob down. A female police officer came over to pat Jana down.

"You may go in now," the first officer said. "Do you need an escort?"

"No, we'll be fine," Jacob replied.

The higher-ups, both in the CIA and the Israeli police, had decided not to spread the information that some radical group might be looking for the Ark on the Temple Mount. Jana got the impression that neither party fully accepted the idea, and the police at the gate never let their guard down in any case.

She and Jacob would handle this themselves. If they needed the police, they were only a shout away.

"There's a surveying crew inside," the cop said. "Don't mind them. They've been working here for some time, getting ready for some restoration work. They're being watched over by a representative of the Waqf."

This was said with a note of contempt. The Jerusalem Islamic Waqf was an old organization, responsible for overseeing the religious site ever since the Muslims reconquered Jerusalem from the Crusaders in 1187. It had gone through many permutations over the centuries as the area changed hands between various Islamic empires, and at the time of the foundation of Israel, the Waqf was overseen by the Jordanian government, which controlled the Temple Mount and all of East Jerusalem.

After the 1967 war pushed the Jordanians out of all the lands west of the River Jordan, the Israelis, in order to keep the peace with the large Muslim population it inherited in East Jerusalem and the West Bank, allowed the Waqf, still under Jordanian authority, to continue to oversee the site.

They tended to be highly protective of the site's Muslim heritage, almost to the exclusion of both other major religions. Jana didn't envy the restoration crew having to work under their eagle eye.

"All right, we'll try to stay out of their way," Jacob said.

Just then, someone called out in American English. "Hey, Mitch! Is that you?"

Jana wouldn't have paid attention except she saw Jacob's jaw tighten. He passed through the metal gate. Jana followed, glancing over her shoulder. She saw a man in civilian clothing, with the muscles, bearing, and buzz cut of a military man, grinning and waving at them. "Mitch!"

He moved forward. A policeman restrained him.

"No, no. Wait in line."

"Mitch! Hey lady, could you tell Mitch it's Sergeant Louis Kenner? We served together."

Jacob kept on going. Jana looked away from the sergeant and followed, her mind swirling. *Mitch? Is that your real name? Or were you lying about your name in the military?*

She knew that she wouldn't get an answer, so she didn't ask.

They passed through a metal gate and entered the Temple Mount.

Jana took in a sharp breath and paused, the strange incident of a moment before forgotten. No matter how many times she entered this place, it still struck her as much as it had the very first time.

Much of the Temple Mount was a broad open area, a relief for the eye after the narrow and crowded streets of the Old City. The view was dominated by the Dome of the Rock, an exquisite octagonal building of blue, green, and yellow tile with intricate Arabic calligraphy all around it and surmounted by a gold dome that could be seen from across the city. It had been built in 692 AD in the early days of Muslim rule, and partially rebuilt in 1023. It was one of the most stunning works of architecture Jana had ever seen, and she had seen most of the great monuments of the world.

It covered an outcropping of stone, part of the original hill, the spot where Mohammed is said to have ridden a winged horse up to heaven. The imprint of the horse's hoof could be seen in the stone.

This miracle made it the third holiest spot in Islam after Mecca and Medina.

Off to one side stood the Al-Aqsa mosque, a huge mosque of the eleventh century that if it stood anywhere except in the shadow of the Dome of the Rock, would be considered a masterpiece of architecture. It fit thousands of worshippers for Friday noon prayers, the holiest day for Muslims. In fact, the entire Temple Mount often housed worshipers, sometimes as many as 300,000 bowing to Mecca under the noonday sun. A large fountain stood right in the middle for their ablutions.

Jana turned to Jacob and found him studying everything with a professional eye. He had no time for architectural beauty or the dramatic sweep of history. For him, this was nothing more than a potential battlefield.

That seemed sad to her. He was better traveled than most people could ever hope to be, and yet he got to enjoy so little of it.

"Where do we start?" she asked. "And what do we look for?"

"No idea," he admitted.

"I think I saw a sign over there saying 'This way to the Ark.'"

"Har har."

They looked around again. She noticed several men in reflective vests and hard hats working in scattered areas of the site. One had set up a theodolite and was looking through it while another one, standing some distance away, held up a measuring rod. Some more were unloading a box of tools in another part of the Temple Mount, and three more were walking near the Dome of the Rock, a Muslim cleric trailing them.

"I say we split up," Jacob said. "This place is huge, and we don't have much time. Keep an eye out for anything that strikes you as unusual, anything that seems out of place."

"Jacob, people have been looking for hidden entrances on the Temple Mount for centuries. I'm not going to find anything."

"You might spot something that has changed. Perhaps these guys left a mark somewhere, or some religious items as a blessing or something."

"Oh, I see what you mean. Several years ago, some ultra-Orthodox Jews came up here and laid a foundation stone, claiming they were starting the Third Temple."

"I'm sure that went over well with the Muslims."

"About as well as it did with the Jews. The Third Temple isn't supposed to be founded until the coming of the Messiah. The rabbis denounced them for sacrilege, and the police arrested them for disturbing the peace."

"OK, let's get to work. I'll check that way, toward the Al-Aqsa mosque, you go to the other end of the Temple Mount, and we'll work our way toward each other and meet in the middle. Call me if you spot anything."

"All right."

They split up. Jana headed for the edge of the Temple Mount, where the enclosure wall hugged close to the steep slope heading down. Since the entire area inside the enclosure was paved, she figured that the only place to see the original surface, besides the stone inside the Dome of the Rock, was at the base of the old wall where it met the ground. Perhaps that area, with its peek at the past, might have attracted the gang that had killed her colleague.

But she was soon to be disappointed. The wall was seamlessly connected to the paving stones. At no point did the original ground show through.

So, she changed her tactic, studying each paving stone as she walked along for signs that it had been pried up or marked.

Nothing. Ten minutes of nothing.

This is getting frustrating.

She checked her watch. If they wanted to find any clues, they needed to hurry before the tourist hordes stormed in.

Jana stopped again and looked around. Luckily, the only other people here yet were the workmen. Maybe she should ask them.

She spotted two of them, followed by the Muslim cleric, enter a ten-foot-long prefab building of the kind often found on worksites. She strolled over, casting a curious glance over at the surveying team. The man with the measuring rod had dropped it with a clack, and he and the man at the theodolite hurried over to a stack of scaffolding tubes.

Jana continued to the prefab. Just as she got there, the two workmen came out. The Muslim cleric did not.

She stopped short just a few paces from them, her senses tingling.

What was it that warned her? The fact that both men looked a bit flushed? The fact that the one coming out last was reaching for the door as if to shut the old Muslim man inside? The faint sound coming from within, as if of someone choking?

But what really froze her to the spot was the way they looked at her, with a mixture of surprise and anger.

She turned to run, at the same time reaching in her pocket for her phone.

They ran after her.

"Jacob!" she shouted.

But the Temple Mount was too big. Jacob was out of sight. He couldn't see the men run her down after only a few steps, pin her arms to her sides, and clamp a hand over her mouth.

He didn't hear her either.

CHAPTER TWENTY

Jacob glanced at his watch, growing increasingly frustrated. He wasn't finding anything, and he got the feeling that he wasn't going to find anything.

Maybe wandering aimlessly around the open areas was the wrong approach. The entire surface seemed to be covered with flagstones, sealing off what lay beneath. The only place he knew of where the original surface showed through was in the Dome of the Rock. He remembered seeing, on a rare day off in Jerusalem during a mission a few years back, the outcropping of stone Mohammed was supposed to have touched.

Maybe the radical group figured that since that was the holiest spot, it was some sort of gate to the tunnels below?

A longshot, but this whole mission had been a longshot since the start. Not even Jana's expertise was helping them much.

Damn, what did she think about Louis spotting him at the gate? Of all the people to bump into! No way was she going to buy that halting coverup. He'd been as obvious as hell.

He felt bad for Louis too. The guy looked hurt when he had ghosted him like that.

And Jana was going to have some serious questions about his past, questions he couldn't answer.

Never mind that now. Time was ticking. Even the work crew was in a hurry before the crowds started to come in. They were grabbing tubes of scaffolding and placing them up against Al-Aqsa Mosque as well as the Dome of the Rock. Jacob nodded to one man standing near the entrance to the Dome of the Rock, who nodded back as he talked quietly on a walkie talkie.

Jacob entered through a graceful arch of intricate blue and green tile supported by marble columns and entered the interior.

Inside, it was all one large room, an octagonal space enclosing a circular arcade of marble columns supporting a stunning façade of elaborate gold scrollwork. The interior of the dome rose above in a dizzying display of gold calligraphy.

Beautiful, but he forced his eyes downward, to what the Muslims found far more important, a plain outcropping of rock about twenty-feet-wide and thirty-feet-long. A chunk of the hill's original bedrock.

He went to the railing and peered over the edge. The base of the building rested right on the stone. He didn't see any gaps at all.

Damn. He began to move slowly around the circle, checking every inch. There had to be an opening somewhere.

Or maybe there wasn't. Maybe, like he had suspected before, that ANFO was to blast in a certain spot in order to gain access to the tunnels that supposedly lay beneath.

But where? He was hoping the group had been here already and had marked the spot somehow. But what if they hadn't? What if they hadn't even arrived yet?

Jacob was so intent on searching the holy stone that he didn't notice a figure slip through the doorway and dart between the columns.

Not at first. But then his peripheral vision caught the movement, and he whirled around.

Too late. The man who had been talking on the radio stepped out from behind a column, gripping a Galil. The compact submachine gun pointed right at him.

Jacob threw up his hands.

"Sorry, officer! I was just looking. I'm an archaeologist. I wasn't going to touch anything. I care about the ancient sites just as much as anybody."

Jacob knew this guy wasn't a police officer any more than he was an archaeologist.

He'd found the radicals. Or more precisely, one of the radicals had found him.

The man paced forward.

"Hold on! I have a permit to be here. I'm not trespassing."

Jacob said all this in English, playing the part of the clueless American, a trick that had put potential adversaries off guard on a number of occasions.

Not this time.

"What's your religion?" the man demanded. He spoke English with a German accent.

My religion? Oh. Guess right, buddy.

Muslim? This guy doesn't look Muslim.

Jewish? Damn, I wish I still had Feinstein's Star of David. But if I say I'm Jewish, he might ask me questions I can't answer.

"I'm Christian."

"What's your background?"

The man stood close now, almost close enough to reach out and grab.

Almost, but not quite. This guy had training.

"My background? I got a degree at—"

"Your racial background."

Jacob blinked. Then he remembered the work crew all being white. None of them looked like Levantine or North African Jews.

"English and Scottish. My grandpa says we got some Danish too."

The man gave a curt nod.

"Come with me. Don't try anything, and I won't hurt you."

Oh, but I'm *going to hurt* you, *my white supremacist friend.*

Because now he understood. The Nazis had always had an obsession with ancient religious artifacts, even those from "inferior" religions such as Judaism. Even some of the highest-ranking leaders of the Third Reich had been entranced by occultism and ancient mysteries.

But what exactly did these guys want?

The man stepped aside to allow Jacob to pass, giving him too much room. Jacob bided his time.

"What's going on?" Jacob asked, keeping his hands up.

"Face forward and walk slowly."

Jacob did what he was told. "What's going on?" he asked again.

"History in the making," the man said in tones hushed by awe.

A radical, all right, just not the kind of radical we expected.

Jacob thought fast. The man was leading him to a far corner of the building, opposite from the doorway.

"Look, I didn't mean any harm. I'm just an archaeologist investigating some subsurface anomalies."

"Subsurface anomalies?"

"Yeah," Jacob said, remembering something Jana had said about her excavation in Morocco. "We use ground-penetrating radar to find foundations of old buildings under the soil. If we turn up the power, we can penetrate rock. We found evidence for some tunnels here."

"Stop."

Jacob stopped.

"Turn around."

Jacob did so.

The man stared at him with a mixture of hope and mistrust. “You found evidence of tunnels? Really? Do you have any printouts of the scan?”

“My colleague has them,” Jacob said, still biding for time.

God, have they captured Jana yet?

“So, the tunnels really do exist,” the man whispered in German. Another of the several languages Jacob spoke.

“What did you say?” Jacob asked.

“Nothing. Keep moving.”

“I found some evidence of an entrance,” Jacob said, turning and pointing. “Right over there.”

The bad thing about radicals was that they were so bound up in their belief system that they’d kill anyone who got in their way. The good thing about radicals was that they were so bound up in their belief system that they were really gullible.

The German turned to look.

Fast as lightning, Jacob moved in.

The German realized his mistake a half second after his eyes shifted from Jacob. He began to turn back, but by then Jacob’s left hand was striking the barrel of the gun, deflecting it to the side as his right fist went for the guy’s throat.

The German tucked his chin just in time to save his windpipe from being crushed. Instead, he got the full force of Jacob’s punch on the point of his jaw, and he fell backwards, smacking his head against the marble floor.

He hadn’t even had a chance to let off a burst from his submachine gun.

Jacob snatched it, pointed it at the groaning man at his feet, and paused. He glanced at the rock, then at the dome and the verses of the Koran inscribed in gold encircling the dome.

His finger eased off the trigger.

Jacob knelt, gave the guy a gut punch to keep him civil, and pulled out a couple of zip ties he kept in his vest pocket for such an occasion.

Within a few seconds, the German was trussed like a Thanksgiving turkey, just like Jana a few days before. A quick pat down brought up nothing except some car keys and a spare magazine. Jacob pocketed them both.

“What are your plans? How many of you are there?”

The guy only replied with a few choice words in German.

Jacob didn't waste his time. His prisoner was probably too crazy to break, and Jacob didn't have the time to test that.

Gagging the German with one of the guy's own socks, he left him.

He got to the entrance to the Dome of the Rock and peeked out.

Two of the "restoration crew" stood at the far end of the enclosure with their backs to him, laying scaffolding tubes end to end, connected with wires.

The ANFO must be in those tubes. They've created a string of pipe bombs.

Jacob moved a little farther out and saw the pipes running around much of the edge of the enclosure.

These guys work fast.

The two he could see still had their backs turned and were far away. Jacob took a chance and slipped out of the entrance, running around the outside of the building until he came into view of Al-Aqsa Mosque.

There he froze. The entire front façade was ringed with scaffolding tubes. A long wire snaked across the ground to connect with the tubes set along the enclosure wall.

If they set that off, they'll blow half the Temple Mount away. The Muslims will blame the Jews, and the Jews will blame the Muslims.

Millions will die.

But I thought these guys were trying to get under the Temple Mount, not blow it up.

I've got to find Jana!

Before he got the chance to do anything, movement toward the security gate they had come through caught his eye.

One of the construction workers pushed a small dolly with a short section of tubing on it toward the entrance and let go. The smooth flagstones allowed the dolly to speed toward the entrance. There was a shout from the guards on duty and everyone took cover. The man pulled out a controller and pushed a button.

The ANFO pipe bomb detonated just as the dolly took it under the arch.

The explosion ripped through the air. Chunks of the historic arch broke off. The metal gate stayed intact, but the bulletproof glass of the guard station spiderwebbed and crumpled.

Jacob couldn't see if there were any casualties. All the Israeli police had ducked out of sight.

As screams filled the air, another of the terrorists that Jacob couldn't see called out on a megaphone in Hebrew. "We have the

Temple Mount set to blow. If anyone fires on us, we will destroy the entire place. If anyone tries to enter any of the gates, we will destroy the entire place. If any drone, airplane, or helicopter flies over our position, we will destroy the entire place. Stay where you are and await further instructions."

Jacob sprinted back to the shelter of the Dome of the Rock, praying he hadn't been spotted.

CHAPTER TWENTY ONE

Jana stopped struggling when she saw the dead body on the floor. The Muslim cleric had a piano wire wrapped tightly around his neck, twisted and knotted at the back. He lay on his side, eyes bugged, hands behind his neck where he had tried vainly, with his last strength, to loosen the garotte.

This is how Arnold Woburn died.

Jana glanced around the inside of the prefab work office. A small desk. Some surveying equipment leaning in one corner. A scattering of tools on another desk. A large blueprint of the Temple Mount on one wall.

A small section on the eastern wall, well away from the gates, was circled in red.

That's all she got to see before the man holding a hand to her mouth glared at her and said, "I'm going to take my hand away. If you scream, I'll kill you."

The tall, blond man spoke English with a Scandinavian accent. His cold, blue eyes looked at her without pity.

The second man, who had her arms twisted behind her back, gave them a painful tug to emphasize the point.

The hand came away from her mouth. Jana gasped for air.

"Who are you?" the Scandinavian man demanded.

"I'm an archaeologist. We were given permission to take a look around before the public came in."

"What are you looking for?"

"Traces of the old Temple. There's a theory that the lowest of the steps leading up to the Dome of the Rock is actually the top of one of the old walls. It's ashlar, large blocks, unlike of the surrounding flagstones. We were looking for evidence of more such features."

Her captors looked entirely uninterested in this archaeological trivia. Jana was actually surprised she had come up with it, given the circumstances.

"The man you came in with, is he an archaeologist too?"

"Yes. What's going on?"

"Never mind that. What's your religion?"

Jana paused, sensing her answer might mean the difference between instant death and a stay of execution. She wished she could see under his hard hat to check if he was wearing a kippah.

Although he didn't look ultra-Orthodox. He wore modern clothing and didn't have the traditional ringlets framing his face. The Muslim cleric might have been killed not for his religion, but simply because he was in the way.

"Christian." That seemed the safest bet.

The Scandinavian nodded.

"What's your background?" he asked.

"My background?"

"Your ethnicity."

"English and Dutch. Why?"

"Nothing else?"

"No. Why?"

The Scandinavian smiled. "A pure Aryan woman. A treasure in the debased modern world. You're the future of the master race. And an archaeologist too. Congratulations. You've just earned a front row seat to history. But make no mistake. You are still a hostage, and if you try to make any trouble, we won't hesitate to kill you. Come, there isn't much time. The Jews will plan some trick, as they always do."

Nazis. We've been thinking it was Muslim radicals all this time, and it turns out to be Nazis?

The loud thud of an explosion shook her to her core.

"What was that?" she cried.

"A warning to the Yids," the Scandinavian said as he peeked out the door.

Someone on a megaphone announced in Hebrew, "We have the Temple Mount set to blow. If anyone fires on us, we will destroy the entire place. If anyone tries to enter any of the gates, we will destroy the entire place. If any drone, airplane, or helicopter flies over our position, we will destroy the entire place. Stay where you are and await further instructions."

Jana felt sick to her stomach. Nazis had just taken over the Temple Mount. It was unbelievable, like something out of a collective Israeli nightmare. She didn't even have to be Jewish to be disgusted by the mere idea.

"What are you going to do?" she demanded.

"Keep quiet. You'll see."

The other man spoke for the first time. "Are we really going to bring her along? She'll only get in the way."

"A hostage is always a good idea, and like I said, she's an archaeologist. We've been fumbling along just learning on the way. She has real knowledge."

"Maybe she does, maybe she doesn't. And we already have a hostage. The Jews care way more about their precious Temple than they do about some Christian archaeologist."

"True, but a human shield can come in handy. Let's go."

As Jana suspected, they headed for the Eastern Wall. This wall was the oldest of the walls, and while it had been restored several times, much of it dated to the time of King Hezekiah of Judah in the seventh century BC. Part of it overlooked a steep slope on which there was a Muslim cemetery. It was to this portion that the two Nazis led her.

As they did, Jana took a look around. Scaffolding tubes were stretched around long sections of the Western and Southern walls, as well as the façade of the Al-Aqsa Mosque. Insulated cables connected them all to one another.

Jana didn't need to be a CIA agent to figure out what was inside those metal tubes.

She glanced back at the gate through which they had come, now far behind her. Smoke hung over it like some ominous curtain. Several other men dressed as workers ran around. One had pulled out a large toolbox and was handing out weapons. Others took up positions around the compound, covering all the gates. She could see that the Israeli police had taken up positions, too, but didn't dare move forward.

Most of the false workers headed for the Eastern Wall.

The Scandinavian man got on a walkie talkie. "We have the woman. Has anyone captured the man yet?"

This question was greeted with silence.

"I repeat, has anyone captured the man yet?"

A voice crackled over the radio. "He was near the Dome of the Rock just a minute ago."

"Go get him and take backup."

"Roger."

They arrived at the Eastern Wall. Several of the scaffolding tubes were stacked at one point against the wall with bags of cement piled on top of them.

At first, Jana didn't understand what the bags were for. Then it hit her. Without them, the force of the blast would mostly dissipate in the open air. With their heavy mass on top, more of the force of the blast would go down.

They were going to blast excavate one of the holiest sites in the world.

* * *

Jacob hid inside the entrance to the Dome of the Rock, unsure what to do next. He was outnumbered ten to one, the Nazis could blow the whole area at any moment, and they might have Jana hostage.

Even if they didn't, they'd probably track her down soon.

Track him down too. He and Jana had been wandering around the Temple Mount for a quarter of an hour in clear view of the entire crew. They all knew he was in the compound somewhere, and they'd be coming for him.

Why didn't I suspect the work crew? I'm such an idiot!

But was it really his fault? He had trusted Israeli security to properly screen anyone coming in. This construction company must have been a group of deep moles, working in the country for years and gaining trust.

None of that mattered now. What mattered was how the hell he was going to stop them from starting World War Three.

And he had to do it without firing a shot. Somewhere, one of these guys was hiding out with a remote switch to blow the explosives. If he heard a shot, it would be all over.

The soft sound of footsteps outside the door put him on alert. Although he couldn't be sure, it sounded like two people.

The entrance was a wide one. If they were smart, they'd come from opposite sides so they could back each other up.

And that's exactly what they did.

One swept around the corner right in front of Jacob. The other came around the other corner of the arch, well out of reach.

The close one jabbed at him and Jacob ducked back, feeling a tingle as the Taser in his hand barely missed him. The guy farther away raised a machete and closed in. Both had submachine guns strapped to their backs

They're afraid of shooting too. They don't want to spook their friend.

That gave him an advantage. Sort of. It was still two against one.

The man lunged with the Taser again, and Jacob dodged a second time. Although he held a submachine gun in his hands, Jacob didn't dare try to block with it. A Galil is nearly all metal, and if the Taser hit it, he'd get shocked just as much as if the guy ground it into his flesh.

The two men pursued him. Jacob tried to keep the guy with the Taser between himself and his friend with the machete.

The Nazi lunged a third time, and this time Jacob was ready. Dropping the Galil, he smacked the man's arm away with an instant to spare, got him into an armlock, and twisted.

The Taser fell to the floor, but before Jacob could finish the guy off, he had to let him go as the other one made a vicious swing at him with the machete.

Jacob backed off, getting into a fighting stance.

The man he had disarmed rubbed his arm and took a step toward the Taser. Jacob needed to get rid of at least one of these guys right now.

The man with the machete decided for him by closing in, swiping at his head. Jacob ducked, feeling the wide blade swoosh over his head, then had to back up as the man turned his hand and slashed down diagonally.

The guy was quick, but not as quick as Jacob Snow. As he sliced at him again, Jacob dropped prone, locked his legs around the man's lead leg, and twisted.

The guy fell to the floor, hard enough to stun him for a second but not hard enough to make him drop the machete.

A hammer fist to the temple, which made his head bounce off the marble floor, took care of that. The man went limp.

Jacob had just enough time to spring away before that damn Taser roasted him.

He scrambled to his feet, and the dance resumed. The Nazi circled him, cautious now, and Jacob kept back up, circling, looking for an opening.

"He's in here!" the guy shouted. His words echoed through the dome.

Had they heard? Better not give them a second chance.

Jacob dove in, risking all to chop his hand down on the guy's weapon wrist.

His opponent cried out, and for a second time, the Taser fell to the floor.

Jacob spun and landed a back kick straight to his gut. The man folded and flew back, striking the wall. Jacob scooped up the Taser and jammed it against his chest before he could compose himself. The guy convulsed.

Jacob hit him again, then a third time. He had to make sure.

Grabbing his Galil, he checked the entrance. No one within sight.

Pulling out some more zip ties, he secured both prisoners. The guy he had slammed into the floor was just coming to, but Jacob didn't have time to question him about Jana. The team had been spread out. He might not know where Jana was, and even if he did, he wouldn't give up that information without a struggle. Giving him another zap with the Taser to keep him from raising the alarm, he patted both men down.

On the belt of one of them he found a walkie talkie, a higher-end brand with good range and secured channels. It was switched off, no doubt to keep Jacob from hearing it while they tried to sneak up on him.

He took it and switched it on, keeping the volume low. Just as he did, he missed the tail end of a sentence.

"—ed."

Voice One: "Spotter, you in position?"

Voice Two: "Checked and ready."

Voice One: "Keep an eye on those gates. Dome of the Rock team, you find him?"

Pause. Jacob felt tempted to imitate them, but the sound quality was good on these. Would they notice an unfamiliar voice?

Voice One: "Dome of the Rock Team?"

Remembering something he had learned in Signals training in Ranger training, he yanked out his phone, turned it on, and held it up against the walkie talkie's antenna.

"We're still looking for him," Jacob said.

Voice One: "Repeat? You're breaking up."

Jacob smiled. The RF radiation put out from an average cell phone wreaked havoc with weaker UHF signals.

"He's not in the main area. We're looking in the back rooms," Jacob said, hoping the Dome of the Rock had back rooms. There must be a janitor's closet, right?

Voice One: "All I caught was you're looking. The walls must be too thick for the radio. Keep at it and report back as soon as you can."

"Roger," Jacob said, cutting off the mic halfway through the word.

"Voice One: "All other spots secure?"

Voice Two: "Spotter's station secure."

Voice Three: "North sector secure."

Voice Four: "West sector secure."

Voice One: "Right. Announcer, make announcement number two."

From outside, Jacob heard the man on the megaphone again. "We have seen you massing police at the gates. Stay back. We are letting off a small charge to show we are serious. If you fire or try to advance, we will blow off the main charge."

Damn, what are they going to blow up?

Jacob sprinted out of the Dome of the Rock, looking all around him. All he saw was the low silhouette of someone atop the Al-Aqsa Mosque, positioned right at the back, as far away from the charges on the façade as he could get.

The spotter?

If so, he didn't shout into his walkie talkie that he had spotted Jacob. He was probably focusing on the gate.

That gave him a chance. Just a slim one, but better than nothing.

He darted along, zigzagging, and running low, eyes scanning for the others. He spotted a couple hiding behind a pile of marble tiles, their backs to him and watching the northern gates into the compound. Then he spotted a group lying prone behind some crates near the East Wall.

And against the East Wall was a pile of scaffolding tubes poking out from underneath what looked like a stack of cement mix bags.

Oh, crap.

Jacob dropped to the ground.

Just in time to feel the ground shudder as the Eastern Wall was ripped by an explosion.

CHAPTER TWENTY TWO

Jana screamed even though she knew what was coming. She screamed not out of fear of getting hurt, but from sheer terror at what the desecration of such a holy site would do to the tumultuous situation in the Middle East. This would cause fury on all sides. Even if the Nazis were wiped out and everyone knew that very same day who had done this and why, all the factions would still blame their enemies for the destruction. Thousands would die.

She had to stop them before they did even worse damage.

Jana and her captors peeked over the stack of metal crates, which had shifted and dented from the impact of the explosion. Dust blocked their vision, making them blink and cough. As it slowly cleared, she saw with horror that a five-foot portion of the old wall had collapsed, revealing a view of Jerusalem through a jagged canyon of tumbled stone. At its base yawned a pit several feet deep.

Through the ringing in her ears, she heard a distant shout to her left. She turned and saw that a man who looked and dressed like an American was shouting just a few feet away. She had nearly been deafened by the blast. He waved one arm, and three of the six men with her got up and ran over to the pit. One had a pick, another a crowbar, and the third a shovel.

They got to work. The remaining men—the American giving the orders, the Scandinavian, and the other man who had captured her—arrayed themselves around the area, Galils leveled, keeping a sharp eye out for Israeli interference.

That possibility scared Jana most of all. The Israelis had just witnessed the worst desecration of a Jewish site since Kristallnacht. Would the police have enough discipline to heed the Nazis' warning and keep back? What about nearby Israeli civilians, many of whom carried guns? And what about the Muslim population in the adjoining Old City? Thousands of them had just witnessed the desecration of one of the holiest sites of their religion.

And what about the world? Video of this would hit the Internet within seconds, the news networks within minutes. She envisioned riots from London to Islamabad.

Despite all that, despite her fear that she might be gunned down at any moment, and despite her worries that they must surely be hunting for Jacob, she walked toward the pit as if in a dream. No one tried to stop her.

She got to the edge of the pit, her ankles twisting on the loose rubble, and looked where the three men dug furiously, prying away larger stones and shoveling smaller pieces of rubble out of the way.

One let out a whoop. Jana almost did, too, for at his feet opened a narrow crevasse of darkness.

All three men pulled out straps with headlamps and put them around their hardhats. One knelt down, switched it on, and peered inside the crack.

"We got it!" he shouted. "It's really here! I see a tunnel!"

The other two crowded close. So did Jana. In their excitement, none of them challenged their prisoner at having a view of this historic occasion.

The beams struggled to penetrate the haze of dust that still hung everywhere, but through it she could see a narrow crack through jagged stones, barely big enough to fit through. The space opened up about ten feet down. The view was too narrow to really tell, but it looked like it opened into a corridor.

Jana shuddered, overcome with that rarest of emotions—awe.

The American leader rushed over, strapping on his own headlamp. The Scandinavian stood in the background, shouting happily into his walkie talkie.

"You were right, Carl!" one of the workers shouted. "There really are tunnels down there."

This was said to the American, who gave Jana a sidelong look.

A chill washed over her. The man had slipped and revealed his leader's name. She would not be allowed to live.

The Scandinavian rushed up. "Let's get in there. We don't have much time before the Jews try something."

Carl pointed at Jana. "We need to deal with her first."

Jana prepared to run, to grapple with her abductors, anything but meekly die at their filthy hands, but then the Scandinavian surprised her.

"We should take her along. She says she's an archaeologist. She might come in handy."

"Is she racially pure?"

"She says so."

Carl looked at her sharply for a moment, then nodded. "All right."

"You sure?" another American asked him.

"Yes, I'm sure." Carl sounded irritated, as if he had had to deal with questions from this man on a regular basis, and it annoyed him. "I go first."

Carl slung his Galil and sat on the edge of the crevasse. Bracing his arms on either side, he began to worm his way down, releasing a cascade of smaller stones as he did so.

Jana watched, as entranced as the rest of them as he descended lower and lower and dropped the last few feet to a floor cut from the living rock of the hill.

He paused there for a moment.

"What do you see?" one of his followers asked.

"A corridor," he said, his voice so hushed with awe that Jana barely heard him. "A corridor that branches off after a few paces. Get down here! All of you!"

"No way!" the American said and started wriggling down the narrow space.

Another man went next, then the Scandinavian gestured to Jana with his gun. Heart beating fast, Jana lowered herself into the gap.

It was a tight fit for her, so for the larger men, it must have been nearly impassable. Gritting her teeth, elbows and knees banging against stone and hands getting scraped, she managed to pick her way down, half climbing, half sliding, until her feet touched nothing but air. She shimmied down a little farther before the strain made her let go.

She smacked her jaw against a stone, clenching her eyes shut, then fell on her feet on a flat surface.

Rubbing her jaw, she opened her eyes and looked around.

She found herself at the dead end of a corridor that stopped at the old wall behind her. Ahead, the corridor, hewn from the hillside and about five feet wide and six feet high, ran straight ahead for about twenty yards before branching to the left and right. It also continued straight ahead as far as the weak lights of the headlamps penetrated.

Carl stood in the intersection, peering down each option in turn. He turned to her. "Which way do we go?" he asked her. "Which way is it?"

"I don't know."

"Subsurface imaging must have detected this," Carl said. "The Jewish government must know about this."

“They must,” Jana agreed. This was the biggest archaeological coverup in history.

“So, what are they hiding down here?” Carl asked. “Is the Ark really here?”

She had no answer and realized that, despite the danger, she wanted to know just as much as they did. Slowly, as if in a dream, she walked to the intersection. The Scandinavian joined her as the rest of the men scrambled down from the surface.

The Scandinavian’s radio crackled. Fragments of words came through the static. He pulled the radio from his holder.

“What was that?”

“. . . -uy . . . of the . . . after . . . -sue.”

“What? We’re below ground, and it’s breaking up your signal.”

“. . .”

“I should go back up,” he said.

“No,” Carl said. “We need you. You know the history better than anyone except maybe her.”

The Scandinavian handed the radio to one of the others. “Go back up and find out what’s going on.”

The man hurried back down the corridor.

Jana looked down each of the three options. To her right, the corridor lead into a small chamber after a few yards. It entered at the corner of the chamber and therefore, she couldn’t see the room as a whole, or anything in it.

To her left, it ran for about ten yards before ending in a T intersection.

Straight ahead, it continued out of sight, with side corridors at regular intervals.

“Jesus,” Carl said. “We’re in a damn maze!”

“We need to get farther down,” the Scandinavian said. “The base of the temple is at a much lower level. It was built on a lower portion of the hill to the west. We need to find some stairs or a ramp.”

Carl turned to Jana, pointing his gun at her. “Do you think that’s right?”

“How should I know? It makes sense, but it’s impossible to know for sure.”

Carl grinned. “I know we’re going to find it. It’s our destiny. We were right about these tunnels, weren’t we? Years of research went into this, delving through esoteric works and travelers’ tales from hundreds of years ago. We’ve found the tunnels, and now we’re going to find the

Ark of the Covenant and the Rod of Aaron. Come on guys, let's check each of these side passages, but don't get out of shouting distance. We want to stick together as much as we can." He jerked his gun at Jana. "Get ahead of me. We're going straight ahead to see what we can find. And you better get more helpful. I don't like killing Aryans, but I will if you get in my way."

As they moved forward, she took a look over her shoulder. Carl was walking a couple of paces behind her. The rest of the team split up along the various branches, and within moments, they were alone.

That gave her a chance. A slim chance, but she needed to take it.

Because she'd rather die than let these lunatics destroy any more of this ancient wonder.

Because every stone they destroyed and every artifact they looted would mean more chaos in the Middle East and more innocent people dying.

CHAPTER TWENTY THREE

Jacob sprinted for the scene of the explosion, every step sending a jab of pain up his leg. The wound he sustained in Algeria, while shallow, had never had a chance to heal, and now the pain and fatigue were catching up with him at the worst possible time.

That wasn't the only thing catching up with him. A couple of the fake work crew were running in his direction, one shouting into a walkie talkie.

Both had guns but neither fired, trapped by their own threat to blow the main charge if the demolition man heard any shots. Jacob supposed he had a radio, too, that they could warn him, but if they started firing, the Israelis might panic and come charging in. And if that happened, they'd have no choice but to blow the main charge.

Once they did that, the Israelis would show no mercy.

So, the two guys bearing down on him would have to kill him with the weapons they carried—one had a long knife and the other had a hammer.

And he couldn't fire back either, not without kicking off World War Three.

He was almost to the scene of the blast. Now, he could see that there was a deep hole and a dark pit at the bottom of it.

He got to the edge just ahead of his pursuers and looked down.

A narrow rift in the stone led down to a more open area. He couldn't see more because a man in a hard hat stood directly below him, holding a walkie talkie to his ear.

"He's right above you!" a voice on the radio shouted.

The man looked up, eyes going wide, his mouth forming an O.

Jacob stepped off into air, bringing his arms up to protect his face.

He plummeted straight down, bashing against the side of the crevasse, bumping his back and both elbows before his feet slammed hard against the man's shoulders.

Both men fell to the floor. Pain lanced up through Jacob's leg, and he toppled to the side, banging his shoulder against the wall.

The man he had landed on groaned, trying to rise.

Jacob didn't give him that chance. He gave him a punch straight to the Adam's apple, crushing his throat in on itself. He had hesitated about killing in holy sites just a few minutes before, but now that they were blasting the place, he figured anyone in higher authority would forgive him.

He tried to rise, hissed in pain, and fell on his ass. Cursing, he got on his hands and knees, grabbed the wall, and managed to stand as the guy he fell on choked to death.

Only then did Jacob realize just what a crappy situation he was in. Above, both men stood staring down at him, not daring to shoot but blocking his escape. Ahead, stretching into the darkness, ran a network of passages. A light bobbed far ahead, and light sources came from corridors leading to either side, but the nearest portions were swathed in shadow.

The guy at his feet had a headlamp around his hard hat, but it had broken in his fall.

Of course it did. That's just my kind of luck.

He picked up and checked his Galil to make sure it looked functional and stared up at the two guys looking down at him.

Surreal. Almost at point-blank range and neither side dared take a shot.

Jacob flipped them off and hobbled down the tunnel.

"The male archaeologist is in the tunnel!" one of the men guarding the exit shouted down. The warning echoed through the darkened corridors.

Damn. He needed to move fast.

The light far ahead of him turned in his direction. He froze.

"What?" a voice called from it.

The men on the surface didn't respond. They must not have heard. The light turned away. Whoever was over there must not have seen him, or thought he was one of the team. Jacob would have only been visible as a silhouette, if at all.

A light to the left of the nearby intersection grew brighter, however. Jacob pulled out the Taser and hurried to the corner as fast as his injured leg could carry him.

Just in time. A man came around the corner, carrying an assault rifle. For a brief moment, his headlamp glared in Jacob's face, then swung down as he got the Taser in his gut. The man convulsed and fell. The electronic *zzzt* of the police weapon sounded too damn loud in the corridor.

Jacob was all out of zip ties so there was nothing he could do about this guy except eject the magazine from his Galil, eject the round from the chamber, and take both.

He didn't even have time to check if the guy had a backup before the men at the entrance called out their warning again. Jacob switched off his victim's headlamp.

Down the opposite corridor, he saw lights bobbing, approaching from a chamber there.

He grabbed the headlamp off the man's helmet and ducked round the corner.

Of course, that put him in view of the man or men who had gone straight ahead, but that light had diminished almost to nothingness.

Then from that direction came a jubilant cry, "It's here! I found the staircase!" someone with a Scandinavian accent shouted.

And from around the corner, where whoever had been in the chamber was now approaching, their lights shining on the corridor, a whisper, "Gerald. Look."

The lights focused on the guy Jacob just took out of action.

"Watch out!" the pair at the entrance shouted again. "He's in the tunnel!"

The guys just around the corner would definitely hear that.

Time to take a chance.

Jacob swiveled around the corner, coming low, aiming up to jab his Taser into the man in front . . .

. . . and came up a few inches short. He had misjudged the distance for the both of them.

They both had Galils in their hands. The man in front jabbed at Jacob's face with the butt, and Jacob had to dodge back to avoid getting his skull cracked open like a walnut.

"I'll get him, Gerald," the man behind said, leveling his assault rifle.

Gerald didn't listen, whether because he was fighting for his life or because he thought his buddy firing so close to the entrance was a dumb idea. Either way, that suited Jacob just fine. As Gerald swung at him again, Jacob dodged, waited until Gerald brought the gun to a stop to swing back with a backhand, then touched the end of his Taser against the metal.

Gerald went stiff, hand gripping the metal of his gun, the current flowing through him. The man behind edged around him in the narrow corridor to get a clear shot. Jacob released the Taser and gave Gerald a kick right into his friend.

The second man's Galil let off a single shot, its sound muffled because Gerald had fallen right against the muzzle. Blood spurted from his shoulder as the bullet tore through muscle and bone, flying out to crack against the wall right by Jacob.

As Gerald fell, Jacob dove forward and jammed the Taser in the second man's face.

Down for the count.

Jacob tensed. Had anyone upstairs heard that impulsive idiot's shot? The two men guarding the entrance had stopped shouting. Were they waiting for the entire Temple Mount to detonate, praying that the walls were too thick, the crevasse too small to let the sound out enough for it to carry to the spotter atop Al-Aqsa Mosque?

After a moment, Jacob, and probably them, began to breathe easier. They were still alive.

Not the two men at his feet, not for long. Jacob pulled a utility knife from Gerald's toolbelt and slit their throats with ruthless efficiency. Gerald also had a backpack. Jacob flipped him over, shucked it off, and opened it.

Several small plastic packs of ANFO, plus a detonator and timer, all primed and ready to go.

Jacob grinned, zipped up the backpack again, and put it on his own back.

What to do next? Everyone had gone silent. He looked over at the first man he had Tased and saw him lying still.

Jacob didn't buy that act for an instant. A strong young guy like that should be moving around, getting reoriented and shouting for his friends.

This guy was playing possum.

Crouched low, bloody knife in one hand and a Galil strapped across his back, he stalked toward him.

Just as he got to the intersection, a shot from the far corridor rang out. Someone down there realized that they couldn't hear shots on the surface. This game just got a whole lot nastier.

Jacob leapt past the open space to the safety of the other side. The guy who had been shamming rose up and punched him in the balls.

Pain paralyzed him for a critical moment, and the guy grabbed his knife hand, twisting, trying to get Jacob to drop the weapon.

Jacob forked the fingers of his free hand and jabbed them in the guy's eyes.

He cried out, letting go of Jacob to clutch at his eyes.

An automatic reaction and a fatal mistake. Jacob's knife lodged in his throat a moment later.

Another one down, but there was at least one more down here, the guy with the Scandinavian accent. Not to mention the two at the entrance, who weren't going to hang out up there for the whole fight. Sooner or later, they'd get bold enough to come down.

Jacob eased over to the corner and paused, listening. Faint sunlight filtered down from the direction of the entrance, and artificial light came from the other direction. He heard whispering both ways.

He glanced back toward the corridor he had entered. It ended not far beyond at a T intersection. There were enough headlamps on the dead men to illuminate it and also give him something to see with a little beyond.

Time to flank these guys. They wouldn't wait forever. Soon, they'd try to converge on him.

He moved to the T intersection and gave a quick glance both ways.

To the left, it ended at the wall just like the place they had come in. Had these tunnels been open to the air at some point before being covered over by the Eastern Wall?

That was a question for an archaeologist, and the only one he knew had vanished.

Jacob tamped down the fear that rose in his heart at wondering what might have happened to her.

A corridor ran to the right. In the distance, he could see the faintest glimmering of a light, probably one of the Nazi's headlamps.

As stealthily as possible, Jacob trotted down the corridor, ignoring side passages and pausing every now and then to listen. He did not turn on his own headlamp. He knew their position, and they only had a vague idea of his own. He wanted to keep it that way.

Assuming one or more of them weren't lying in wait in the darkness. Assuming they didn't shift position.

After about twenty yards, he stopped. The faint light ahead dimmed, then slowly faded away, leaving him in darkness.

CHAPTER TWENTY FOUR

Jana choked and struggled as Carl put her in a headlock.

"That's no archaeologist hunting us," he growled. "And you're not either. Who are you? Mossad?"

"We are archaeologists," Jana gasped. "My colleague was a US Marine. He fought in Iraq."

"And you?"

"I'm an archaeologist, like I told you."

"Bullshit," the Scandinavian. "Kill her now."

"No, she's a good hostage."

"The Jews won't care about her."

"No, but he obviously does. Let's get to the staircase."

"It's over here." The Scandinavian pointed to a side passage.

They went over to it, Jana stumbling as Carl kept her in a headlock. Their lights revealed a long, narrow staircase plunging down into the darkness.

"Let's go," Carl said.

"What about the others?" the Scandinavian asked.

"They can take care of themselves. There's not much time." Carl started to descend.

"But—"

"If we wield the Rod of Aaron, we can defeat them all. Bring down the power of heaven to aid God's true people, the Aryan race."

Carl released her and jammed the muzzle of his gun into her back.

"I got to admit," the Scandinavian said with a smile, pushing Jana ahead of him down the stairs, "I didn't fully believe it until I found those references in the archives. Even then I had doubts. But now . . ."

Jana felt the same. Over the course of her career, she had heard all sorts of theories about what lay under the Temple Mount, but she had assumed there was nothing but a solid hill and the ruins of the Temple itself. Now, she knew the hill was honeycombed with tunnels, and surely some of these tunnels, which looked excavated a long time ago, must connect with the Temple on its western slope.

And this staircase, which still led them down, would take them to it.

Because it led to the west, toward the side of the Mount where the Herodian extension to the Temple had stood.

And within that extension lay the foundations for the original Temple of Solomon.

And what was below that?

Down they went, taking care on worn steps that had probably not heard footfalls for a thousand years or more.

But who knew? Surely the Israeli government had discovered this place. Had they sent a secret exploratory mission down here? Or had they sealed it up out of religious respect, never to know its secrets?

At last, the staircase stopped at a chamber deep underground. The air here was musty and stale. Jana wondered when a human being had last taken a breath inside this space.

As Carl and the Scandinavian shone their headlamps around, Jana felt a prickling on her flesh. They were in a chamber about twenty feet wide by forty. A large, gold menorah was in a niche in the wall. All around the top of the wall was a lengthy inscription in ancient Hebrew. She recognized verses from the Torah but didn't have time to read them.

She was too distracted by the bricked-up doorway at the far end of the chamber.

Slowly, the two men walked forward. For the moment, they had forgotten her, entranced by the evidence that they were on the threshold of what they had sought for so long.

They weren't the only ones. Jana stood staring, almost hypnotized by that simple brick wall and what it might signify.

"What does it say?" Carl whispered, pointing to an inscription above the doorway.

The Scandinavian answered. "Any man or woman who breaks the seal shall be smote down by the wrath of Yahweh. The land of Israel will swallow them."

Carl laughed. "If the Jews think God will protect the Ark from his true people, they're going to get a rude wakeup call."

The two men gave each other a high five.

The Scandinavian took off his backpack and pulled out a pickaxe with a short handle.

"Use the shaped charge," Carl said.

"I don't want to damage the Ark."

Jana eased her way up behind the two men.

"We don't have time for this," Carl said.

"This is simple brick, like they used for their houses. It's pretty brittle. I can break through no problem."

"We don't know when the Jews will make their move."

"At least let me break a hole through the wall and see what we're dealing with. It will only take a moment."

The Scandinavian had slung his assault rifle in order to use the pickaxe. Just as he swung the point down on the brick, Jana grabbed it, flicking off the safety and reaching for the trigger. Even though it was strapped to his back, she could still maneuver a shot into Carl, who stood right beside him.

"Stop right there!" a shout came from behind her. Jana froze for a crucial half second.

Carl turned, saw what she was doing, and gave her a backhand that sent her sprawling.

Two men dressed as workers stood at the bottom of the stairs, aiming their assault rifles at her.

"Nice timing," Carl said. "Did you get him?"

"No. When we heard him run off down the tunnels, we climbed down and looked for him. Couldn't find him, though. We found the stairs instead."

Carl's face turned red. "And you came down here, leaving him between us and the surface? You idiots!"

"But—"

"Get back up there and find him!"

"We just saved your life."

"MOVE!"

Grumbling, the two men ran back up the stairs.

Carl turned and pointed his gun at Jana, who was just picking herself off the floor.

"And you, get over to the far wall and stay there. No, don't try to edge over to the staircase, go to *that* wall. And don't move a damn muscle. You're a good bargaining chip to use on that killing machine upstairs, but if you try anything again, I'll gun you down."

Jana ended up with her back to the wall halfway between the sealed door and the staircase.

The Scandinavian glared at her and smacked at the brick with his pick. A chunk crumbled off.

"Why didn't they seal this better?" Carl asked.

"Why argue with good luck?" the Scandinavian said, smacking another portion of brick away. "I suppose they figured they didn't need to since the tunnel system was already hidden and buried. And maybe they wanted to have relatively easy access to it if they decided to move it to a better hiding place."

The Scandinavian worked up a rhythm, hacking away at the brick as Carl cleared away the rubble and broke off cracked bits of brick with his hands. Every now and then, he glanced over at Jana to make sure she hadn't moved before breaking off more of the crumbly old material.

The sound echoed through the chamber, but beneath that, Jana thought she detected another sound, a softer sound. Like a thud. A few moments later, she thought she heard it again.

And then the two Nazis broke through and she forgot everything except what their headlamps revealed through the dust-filled hole.

It was hard to see. The hole was only as big as her head and her captors stood in the way, but craning her neck and standing on tiptoe, she could see a large rectangular object resting on a pedestal, covered by a large cloth of purple material inscribed with Ancient Hebrew in spun gold. The object looked about three feet tall, three feet wide, and four feet long. Sticking out from the cloth were wooden beams on either side.

The size is about right, and it has staves of shittim wood, just like the Bible describes.

The two Nazis stared, silent and motionless. Jana took a step forward, not to make a play for one of their guns again, but to get a better look.

She could see the cover of purple cloth was raised in the center.

The two golden cherubim on the lid. It must be.

She stood, rooted to the spot, staring . . .

. . . until the spell was broken by a strong hand clamping over her mouth.

CHAPTER TWENTY FIVE

Jacob kept his hand over Jana's mouth as he leveled his Galil with his other hand, aiming for the Nazis as they furiously began widening the breach in the wall.

Jana turned her eyes toward him, recognized his face in the dim light, and shook her head.

Don't shoot? Why the hell not?

Then he saw what was beyond the two men breaking through the brick wall.

No. It can't be.

His finger eased off the trigger. He couldn't shoot, not without the risk of hitting . . .

Is that really what I think it is?

Jacob took a step back, pulling Jana with him. Step by step, the sound muffled by the cracking of the brick and the heavy breathing of the two Nazis, they made their way to the staircase.

One looked over his shoulder just as they made it to the doorway.

"Hey!"

"Run!" Jacob said, pushing Jana ahead of him.

Jana bolted up the stairs. Jacob hurried to follow. He got out of sight just as the Nazi fired a burst, the bullets smacking into the stairs an instant after Jacob rushed up them.

Jacob huffed up several more steps, his injured leg slowing him down, the near darkness making him stumble on the uneven stairs. He heard Jana stumbling up ahead of him.

And then it was suddenly, glaringly bright.

On instinct, Jacob whirled and fired an unaimed burst down the stairs at the Nazi standing with his headlamp pointing up the narrow stairs.

The bullets hit everywhere but where Jacob wanted them to. The Nazi let off a shot as he leapt out of sight. The bullet winged Jacob's shoulder.

Jacob stumbled, sat down, and began crawling up the stairs backwards.

“Are you all right?” Jana called down to him from somewhere up above.

“Barely cut flesh. Yeah, I’m fine.”

Except I’m a sitting duck. Except I can barely walk now.

He continued to crawl up the stairs, using both legs and one hand to move, while training his Galil on the illuminated doorway below.

A shadow moved down there. He let off a burst, the bullets smacking off the chamber floor.

Please don’t let a ricochet hit the Ark of the Covenant. I got enough sins to atone for already.

While he hated sending stray shots down the stairs that might hit something that could very well be an actual legend, he figured self-defense and keeping it out of the hands of white supremacists was probably worth the risk. He was probably going to hell anyway.

The Nazis didn’t appear. Jacob continued his awkward progress up the stairs. He slipped on a worn step and banged his injured leg, hissing with pain.

Then a strong hand grabbed him by the strap on his backpack and hauled him along.

With Jana’s help, he managed to move faster, still training his Galil on the doorway. He fired another shot to keep their heads down. In response, one of them reached out with his Galil, not showing his head but only his arms, and fired blind at full auto.

“Jesus!”

Bullets cracked all around them: on the stairs, the walls, and the ceiling. He heard Jana cry out. He fired back, also missing.

The Nazi ran out of ammo and pulled back to reload.

If Jana was hurt, she wasn’t hurt badly. She kept hauling him up by the strap of his backpack.

His backpack! He’d taken it off one of the bodies, and it contained a charge of ANFO with a detonator.

“Let go of me!” Jacob shouted.

“I’m helping you.”

He handed her the Galil. She fumbled for it in the near darkness.

“Here. Fire down there every few seconds to keep them back. Go slow with the ammo. We don’t have much more.”

“What are you going to do?”

He didn’t answer. Instead, he shucked off his pack and unzipped it.

Jana fired. He ignored that, focusing on what he needed to do.

He felt the packs of ANFO, the detonator, and the timer.

Another full burst from the Nazis. Jana and Jacob curled into a tight ball, each trying to protect the other. Even though it was fired blind like before, given the contained area, it was a miracle neither of them got hit.

Again, the Nazi pulled back.

Jacob probed around the timer, not daring to touch any buttons. Why the hell didn't this thing light up?

"Jana, I'm going to have to turn on my headlamp."

"And make ourselves even bigger targets?"

"Yes. Cover me."

He switched on his lamp. Jana fired down the staircase. As quick as he could, he studied the LED display, figured out how to set the timer, glanced up the remaining stairs to gauge how long it would take to get clear, and set the timer for thirty seconds. He switched it on, rose, and stumbled up the stairs, still carrying the bag.

"ANFO?" Jana asked.

"Yep."

"You'll destroy the Ark!" Jana said.

"It's that or let it fall into the hands of Nazis."

"How big of a blast will it make?" She was hauling him up the stairs again.

"Enough to collapse the roof, I hope."

"Don't throw it down on them. I have a better idea. Get to the top of the stairs."

More shots. Behind him, Jana cried out.

He whirled around, stumbled, and fell against the wall.

"You OK?" he asked.

"Shot the gun right out of my hands!"

Jacob switched off the headlamp. The doorway was a pool of light far below.

Twenty seconds.

"Come on!"

He turned and ran.

Only to fall flat on his face. Jana stumbled over him and fell too.

He barely managed to keep a grip on the backpack.

No way we're getting up these stairs without some light.

The Nazis provided it. One of them exposed himself, aimed his beam up the staircase, and fired.

They crawled up the last few steps, making the smallest target possible as more bullets chased them.

Ten seconds.

They got to the top of the stairs. Jana pointed to a niche by the side of the entrance, just visible in the shadowy corridor. If he shoved the pack in there, it would collapse the entrance to the stairway, but the main blast wouldn't hit the tunnel leading down. The Ark, around a corner and across a room, should be all right.

Five seconds.

He shoved the pack in the niche.

"Run!" he shouted.

Jana did as she was told, taking a parting shot as she did.

Sprinting down that corridor was agony. Every time he put weight on his bad leg, he thought it would buckle, sending him flat on his face. They made it around the nearest corner.

The backpack detonated a moment later.

The underground corridor rocked with an ear-spitting explosion. A wave of force blew out of the staircase, sending them rolling over one another and banging them against a wall to lie there stunned.

For a moment, they thought it was over.

Then a loud crash in the staircase told them it wasn't.

Another crash followed the first. Then another, and another. Above them, the ceiling let out an ominous crackling.

Crackling? Given the ringing in their ears, that noise must be as loud as an avalanche if they were hearing it at all.

Jana realized this, too, because she sprang to her feet, grabbed him, and pulled him up.

They stumbled down the corridor together, his headlamp barely penetrating the cloud of dust that rasped their throats and made their eyes water.

A large section of the ceiling tumbled down behind them, collapsing the corridor and sealing the entrance to the staircase.

Coughing and staggering, they made it to the entrance and felt a wave of relief to see sunlight still filtering down. Jacob looked at Jana, saw her covered in dust and almost unrecognizable, and realized that he must look the same.

And that gave him an idea.

He moved over to the bodies.

"Help me get a couple of reflective vests and helmets off these guys."

"That's not much of a disguise."

"We got to take out the demolition guy on the mosque."

"All right. You rest. I'll strip them."

Jacob didn't feel up to objecting. He leaned against the wall, still coughing, not putting any weight on his bad leg, as Jana stripped two bodies and dressed him and herself in the gear.

He looked down at the bodies and laughed. "They're wearing kippahs as a disguise. Nazis pretending to be Jews. That's too much. I need a vacation."

"You need a new lifestyle."

"Big time. Give me a Galil."

She handed him one, plus a spare magazine, and took one for herself.

"These are urban combat guns," he told her. "Not very good at long range. We'll have to get in close."

"Let's go," Jana said, tucking her hair under her helmet. "I'll go up first and help you."

She climbed up, crouched at the top, and Jacob painfully followed, using mostly his arm strength to spare his legs. She helped pull him up the last few feet.

For a moment they lay there, filling their lungs with relatively clean air.

Then Jana flipped over and studied the distant figure atop the mosque. "Is he the last?"

"I don't know. I sure hope so."

"What do we do?"

"The charges are all set in a series. Rigged to explode remotely. I noticed that the detonator is against the Western Wall. If I disable it, none of the bombs will blow."

"Are you sure? Wouldn't he have the detonator by the Al-Aqsa Mosque where he could guard it?"

"Too close to the gates. They wanted to keep it as far away from the police as possible. I'm sure a few of these other guys had remote triggers too."

"God, then I hope he's the last. How are we going to take him out?"

"Later. After I defuse the bomb. You stay here. I'm afraid that he'll see you're too short and slim to be one of his friends."

"If he tries anything, I'll take him out," she said.

"Not from this range. Sit tight."

Jacob got to his feet and unsteadily walked toward the Western Wall. He raised a hand to the distant figure, who returned the wave.

He could just make out that the man raised up a walkie talkie.

Jacob gave an exaggerated shrug, hoping to express that his was lost or broken. He hoped the guy couldn't see Jana too well, half hidden as she was in the pit.

The guy turned back to watch the gates. Good.

The three-minute walk to the Western Wall was the longest walk of Jacob Snow's career. With every painful step, he expected the guy to figure it out and set off the bomb, or for another of his team to intercept him, or the Israelis to finally make some impulsive, foolish move.

None of those things happened.

He got to the cables leading to the regularly-spaced metal tubes filled with ANFO and walked along toward the end. He dared a nervous glance over his shoulder. The guy wasn't looking at him, but rather at Jana's position. He had stood up and looked like he was staring.

Did he suspect that Jana wasn't one of his friends?

Taking the opportunity, Jacob hurried to the end of the cables as fast as he could, got to the detonator, and disconnected it.

He let out a breath of relief.

A distant shout made him turn.

The demolition man had raised a sniper's rifle, pointing straight at him. Sunlight flashed off the scope on top of the rifle.

Jacob knew that he didn't have time to hit the dirt. It wouldn't matter anyway. There wasn't a hiding place for at least twenty yards.

He was a dead man.

A shot rang out across the Temple Mount. The figure atop the mosque twisted and fell over the side. He hit the flagstones and lay still.

Jana walked into view, a Galil in her hands. Jacob gaped.

"A one in a million shot!" Jacob called to her. "Now throw that thing away and let's walk toward the gate with our hands up. Hopefully, our luck will hold, and the cops saw that and won't gun us down."

But, as usual, Jana didn't do as he asked. Instead, she walked over to him and gave him a hug. They stood together for a moment, holding each other up as much as embracing, and then walked toward the gate together.

CHAPTER TWENTY SIX

CIA Jerusalem office
The next morning

Abraham Feinstein smiled at Jacob from across his desk.

"Man, don't you look like a dog's favorite chew toy! Ah, that brings me back. I miss fieldwork."

Jacob smiled. "Well, if I ever get to your age, I hope I'm not saying the same thing."

"You'll see. Have you watched the news coverage?"

"Heavy on the Nazi angle. And the Israelis are spinning it to make it look like they saved the day."

"Sorry about that."

Jacob shrugged. "It's for the best. People would freak if they knew a CIA operative was killing people on the Temple Mount, and Israelis killing Nazis at a holy site is some serious clickbait."

Feinstein nodded somberly. "I think it's saving some lives. Not enough, though, not enough."

All of East Jerusalem and the Palestinian Territories had been convulsed with riots. The ultra-Orthodox had rioted, too, protesting that the government hadn't done enough to secure the holy site. And there had been several major riots in a dozen cities across Europe and the Middle East.

"I did what I could," Jacob said, hanging his head.

"You did, and you did a damn good job, but you know as well as I do that that's not always enough."

Jacob sighed. No, it wasn't always enough.

"Maybe this will cheer you up. Wallace told me to tell you that the Marrakesh mission succeeded. The Moroccans will have a press release in a few days once the hubbub in Jerusalem dies down a bit."

Jacob nodded. "That's a good team over there. I guess they won't get any mention either."

"Nope."

A thought occurred to him. "Was the entrance to the tunnel visible to the camera crews? I didn't see any mention of it on the mainstream media."

"No, the cameras were all pointing from the city, lower down from the hole, so no one saw it. But when you set off that blast inside it created a gust of smoke out of that hole. People saw that on the live stream, and that's been picked up by some conspiracy theorists who have made the right guess for once in their lives. Now some forums are arguing about it, with some people saying it's proof of underground tunnels in the Temple Mount and others saying it was a small detonation."

"Great," Jacob grumbled.

"We've seeded some people into the forums who are claiming there's an alien base down there and that the Second Temple was actually a UFO."

"That'll undercut the conspiracy theorists' credibility!" Jacob said and laughed. "I hope God doesn't get too upset that you're calling him an alien."

Feinstein shrugged and raised his hand to gesture at the space around them. "God has a sense of humor. Look at the world he created."

"You got a point there. Oh, here's your Star of David back. I'm sorry, but I had to put it on a new chain. The old chain got a bullet through it."

Jacob pulled it off and handed it over.

"Oh, it saved you, did it?" Feinstein said with a smile as he put it on.

"That's what an IDF soldier said. Oh, and here's the old chain. You could probably get it fixed if it has sentimental value. I didn't have time. Sorry."

Feinstein laughed. "Sentimental value? I only bought it three months ago after the last guy busted a chain. Interesting story. Wish I could tell it to you."

"I wish I could tell my story."

"You can't, and you won't. How about that archaeologist? Can she be trusted to keep quiet?"

Jacob nodded. "She's Aaron Peters's daughter."

Abraham Feinstein stood. Jacob stood as well. They shook hands.

"That's all you need to say. Good luck to you both."

* * *

Asilah, Morocco
Two days later

Jacob had parked just outside the main gate to the Asilah medina. The medieval city walls and a large, stone tower once used by Raisuli, the last of the Barbary pirates, rose ahead of them. To the west, the Atlantic surf curled against the beach. Children frolicked in the shallows without a care in the world.

The CIA operative stared at them for a moment before turning to Jana. "You sure you don't want me to drive you to the dig site?"

"No. I'll just get a taxi. It's not far. Besides, if you showed up, the crew would ask questions."

Jacob smiled and gestured at her bruised face and scraped hands. "They're going to ask questions anyway."

"I'll say I was in a fender bender in Tangier. It's common enough to be believable."

"All right . . ." Jacob paused, suddenly struggling for words. He looked away, then back at her. "Thanks for all your help. You've been a literal lifesaver. Again."

"Well, I hope that the next time I see you, you won't be tossing grenades around."

"He tossed the grenade. I only tossed it back at him. Plus, I saved your life."

"And I saved your life in Algeria."

Jacob's smile widened. "And Jerusalem. I was as surprised to see you in Algeria as you were to see me on your evening walk. The Marrakesh office has been delving into that, by the way. At the moment, we don't know of any more people gunning for you, and we're still trying to find out why."

"Probably revenge for something my father did."

"Probably. I guess I don't need to tell you that the Moroccan government has a few agents watching the area around your excavation. Even so, I'm glad you're packing up."

"Yeah," she said with a sigh. "I talked to one of my assistants yesterday. They planned to cover over the last of the squares. Other than some lab work and some cleanup, we're done. I'll be back in the States by the end of the week."

"And then what?"

"Processing the finds, applying for more funding, publishing this first season's results, and hopefully coming back here next year. I'm also supposed to consult on a couple of Roman sites in Europe, so I'll be on this side of the Atlantic sometime in the next few months."

She looked at him hopefully. Jacob tensed. "Well, that would be great. If we find ourselves in the same country, maybe we can have a drink or something."

"Without getting shot at?"

"Might make a nice change of pace."

Jana laughed, then grew serious. "I guess I can't have your number."

Jacob shook his head. "No. But I have yours, and I'll call you. And don't forget to call that number I gave you to update us on your movements."

Jana grimaced. "Checking in once a week with the CIA."

"It's for your own protection."

"Yeah," Jana whispered. "I guess it is."

They paused, looking into each other's eyes.

"I guess I better go."

"Yeah. Thanks for everything."

"You too."

Her hand moved a bit toward him, and he turned to more fully face her. Then the hand dropped, she gave an uncertain smile, and got out of the car. She pulled her duffel bag out of the back seat, gave another smile and a brief wave, then hurried off toward the seaside road, where several taxis were lined up.

She got into a taxi, and it drove off. Jacob slumped. That would be the last time he would see her. He'd put her into too much danger already. It wouldn't be fair to involve her more.

He'd protect her, though. Watch over her and root out the people who had tried to kill her. He owed that to Aaron Peters, and he owed that to Jana.

Jacob Snow turned on the ignition and merged with traffic, heading for the Tangier airport. That evening he'd be on a flight to Greece. Back home for some R&R.

Assuming the CIA would allow him to rest.

* * *

Jana sat in the back of the taxi watching the Moroccan countryside roll by, thinking about everything that had happened in the past few days. Of all the danger and all the stunning revelations, one thing kept coming back to her.

That American off-duty soldier recognizing Jacob and calling him Mitch.

The soldier wasn't remembering his name wrong. She could see from Jacob's face that he had revealed something Jacob wanted to remain hidden.

So, he was lying about his name? Why? And if he lied about something so basic, what else was he lying about?

She still didn't know much about Jacob's relationship with her father. They had been close, that was obvious, but had they gone on missions together? Did he know more about Dad's fate than he was telling?

Perhaps if she knew more about him, she'd learn more about her father.

She still had the numbers of some of Dad's old buddies, men who had come to the funeral or who had come to visit earlier on. Some of them had given her their number after Dad died, saying that if she ever needed any help, she could call on them.

While they were mostly retired now, they still might be able to tell her some things. She had never reached out to them before, hating the CIA and how it had taken her father from her, but now that she had been drawn into two different missions and had some mysterious organization gunning for her, she had a reason to ask.

No, she had a *right* to ask.

But would they answer?

She didn't know. Perhaps if she framed it the right way, asked about Jacob—or Mitch or whoever the hell he was—and the attempt on her life, she could find out a bit more about the situation.

And maybe, just maybe, that would lead to some more information about her father.

She looked out the rear window at the tower of Asilah dwindling in the distance, back to where she had said goodbye to Jacob.

This isn't goodbye, Jacob Snow, if that's your real name. I'm not going to wait for you to call me. I'm going to come looking for you, and this time I'm going to be armed with some answers.

* * *

Alpha One sat in his office at The Order's bunker, watching entranced as a live news feed played on his computer screen. A BBC journalist stood on a rooftop in Jerusalem, the Temple Mount in the background.

"Two days on from the attack on the Temple Mount and still no clear answers on how the Aryan Front, a previously unknown neo-Nazi group, had managed to infiltrate the holy site and blow up a portion of the Eastern Wall. While all the terrorists were killed, heavy rioting continues in Muslim and some Jewish neighborhoods in protest of what the rioters see as the Israeli government's lack of vigilance in guarding the site. Latest figures show the death toll from the riots—"

A knock on his door made him switch off the sound.

"Come in."

Gamma Two, his head of external communications, and Delta Four, one of his guards, stood in the doorway with a third man.

This was Omega One, The Order's best undercover operative. An older man in a business suit, features sharp under a shaved head, his icy, blue eyes had a cold stare that could put the fear into many a tough man.

But not Alpha One.

Omega One had been a useful tool, not only for his ability to infiltrate pretty much any secret society, but also for his personal weakness. Omega One loved money. It was always good for one's tools to have a weakness to exploit.

"Thanks for that wire transfer," Omega One said with a grin as he walked in.

"You earned it, having to pretend to be a rich Nazi for the past five years. The company you had to keep must have been unbearable."

"Unbearable but stupid. It was easy to make an excuse so that I didn't have to go along. I just told them the Israelis knew of my sympathies and had me on a watch list. They didn't complain too much considering how much funding I'd given them." Omega One saw what was playing on the screen and gestured to it. "Sorry it didn't go better."

"It went well enough. It caused disorder."

"And disorder is a good thing?"

"Only when it's predictable."

"Who could predict someone would stop them?" Omega One said with a shrug.

"That's not what I'm referring to."

The operative turned to him. "What do you mean?"

"I'm talking about the assassin who got intercepted, the one you arranged through your North African contacts. Only three people knew about him—you, me, and Gamma Two."

Omega One's eyes got shifty. "Oh, well, he might have blabbed."

"Men like him don't blab," Alpha One said and pulled a gun from his desk drawer. "Greedy men like you do, for the right price."

"Wait! Hey! What are you talking about?"

"You're in the pay of the CIA, or some other intelligence agency who tipped off the CIA. How much did they pay you?"

"Don't be crazy. I'd never do that! I make more than enough with you."

"In your mind, there's no such thing as 'more than enough.'"

"Don't shoot! I swear I didn't!"

Delta Four grabbed him from behind, pinned his arms, and cuffed him.

"Oh, I'm not going to shoot," Alpha One said with a smile. "I'm going to let Delta Four and a couple of the other Deltas work on you. We'll find out everything you know."

Delta Four dragged him toward the door.

"Wait! Please!"

"Take your time, Delta Four, and do what you do best. Make sure it lasts a long, long while."

The slamming door cut off Omega One's screams.

Gamma One looked at him, concerned. "What if he compromised the whole operation?"

"I don't think so. He's been feeding little bits of information to get regular payments. It explains a lot of our failed or compromised missions."

"Thank you for not suspecting me. I'm loyal."

"I know. I checked."

Gamma One paled slightly. He cleared his throat and said, "Shall I arrange another assassin to go after Jana Peters?"

Alpha One rubbed his chin. "No, I don't think so. At least not for now. I think I have a better plan for how we can handle that archaeologist. A plan that will achieve even greater results."

NOW AVAILABLE!

TARGET THREE
(The Spy Game—Book #3)

"Thriller writing at its best... A gripping story that's hard to put down."
--Midwest Book Review, Diane Donovan (re Any Means Necessary)

"One of the best thrillers I have read this year. The plot is intelligent and will keep you hooked from the beginning. The author did a superb job creating a set of characters who are fully developed and very much enjoyable. I can hardly wait for the sequel."
--Books and Movie Reviews, Roberto Mattos (re Any Means Necessary)

From #1 bestselling and USA Today bestselling author Jack Mars, author of the critically acclaimed *Luke Stone* and *Agent Zero* series (with over 5,000 five-star reviews), comes an explosive new action-packed espionage series that takes readers on a wild ride across Europe, America, and the world.

Jacob Snow, elite soldier-turned-CIA agent, must race into action when a new terrorist group arises with a terrifying weapon: a deadly disease, lying dormant underwater for centuries. If unleashed, it will wreak unimaginable destruction—and Jacob is the only one who can stop it.

But the path to finding it lies through an ancient relic. And the only one brilliant enough to unravel its symbolism is Jana, Jacob's mysterious partner and archeologist.

Together, they must find and stop the terrorists before its too late. But in a shocking twist, Jacob realizes that his own path may just come back to bring him down.

An unputdownable action thriller with heart-pounding suspense and unforeseen twists, TARGET THREE is the debut novel in an exhilarating new series by a #1 bestselling author that will make you fall in love with a brand-new action hero—and keep you turning pages late into the night. Perfect for fans of Dan Brown, Daniel Silva and Jack Carr.

Future books in the series are also available!

Jack Mars

Jack Mars is the USA Today bestselling author of the LUKE STONE thriller series, which includes seven books. He is also the author of the new FORGING OF LUKE STONE prequel series, comprising six books; of the AGENT ZERO spy thriller series, comprising twelve books; of the TROY STARK thriller series, comprising five books; and of the SPY GAME thriller series, comprising six books.

Jack loves to hear from you, so please feel free to visit www.Jackmarsauthor.com to join the email list, receive a free book, receive free giveaways, connect on Facebook and Twitter, and stay in touch!

BOOKS BY JACK MARS

THE SPY GAME
TARGET ONE (Book #1)
TARGET TWO (Book #2)
TARGET THREE (Book #3)
TARGET FOUR (Book #4)
TARGET FIVE (Book #5)
TARGET SIX (Book #6)

TROY STARK THRILLER SERIES
ROGUE FORCE (Book #1)
ROGUE COMMAND (Book #2)
ROGUE TARGET (Book #3)
ROGUE MISSION (Book #4)
ROGUE SHOT (Book #5)

LUKE STONE THRILLER SERIES
ANY MEANS NECESSARY (Book #1)
OATH OF OFFICE (Book #2)
SITUATION ROOM (Book #3)
OPPOSE ANY FOE (Book #4)
PRESIDENT ELECT (Book #5)
OUR SACRED HONOR (Book #6)
HOUSE DIVIDED (Book #7)

FORGING OF LUKE STONE PREQUEL SERIES
PRIMARY TARGET (Book #1)
PRIMARY COMMAND (Book #2)
PRIMARY THREAT (Book #3)
PRIMARY GLORY (Book #4)
PRIMARY VALOR (Book #5)
PRIMARY DUTY (Book #6)

AN AGENT ZERO SPY THRILLER SERIES
AGENT ZERO (Book #1)
TARGET ZERO (Book #2)
HUNTING ZERO (Book #3)